MARRY ME TWICE

MONICA WALTERS

D1366297

B. LOVE PUBLICATIONS

INTRODUCTION

Hello, Readers!

Thank you for purchasing and/or downloading this book. This work of art contains explicit language, lewd sex scenes, and moments of depression. This is also an insta-love type EROTIC novel. If any of the previously mentioned offend you or serve as triggers for unpleasant times, please do not read.

Also, please remember that your reality isn't everyone's reality. What may seem unrealistic to you could be very real for someone else. But also keep in mind that despite the previously mentioned, this is a fictional story.

If you are okay with the previously mentioned warnings, I hope that you enjoy Haji and Chinara's story.

Monica

 aji

"SHE A FINE MUTHAFUCKA," I said to my friend, Jarius.

"Hell yeah. You gon' holla?"

"Naw. Not today. I met this woman earlier, so I wanna see what she talking 'bout first."

"What if you don't see her again, nigga?"

"She came out of the hair supply store. I'm willing to bet she'll be back in a couple of weeks."

He rolled his eyes as we walked inside his barbershop for him to give me an edge. Just because I was a bachelor didn't mean I had to holla at *every* female I found attractive. Ever since I'd been in the States, though, that reputation followed me. When I got to Lamar University from Sierra Leone, I nearly lost my mind. Being away from the watchful eyes of my parents was like a dream come true. The beautiful women were plentiful, and I made my way through as many as I could my first couple of years in school.

The women loved me. I had dark skin, but it had lightened up some over the years. That African sun hit way different than this American sun. I was motor oil black when I got here. That shit didn't matter, though. They loved my height of six-feet-three inches and, not to mention, all this African dick I was slanging. Just like guys talked about their conquest, so did the ladies. Most of the ones I slept with had approached me. Despite those distractions during the fourteen years I'd been here, I'd obtained a master's degree in chemical engineering.

My dad was pissed. He said I was supposed to come here, get an education, and bring my wealth of knowledge home to my people. Truth was, I loved it here. I'd submerged myself in American culture and absolutely loved southern rap music. As time went on, my accent became more and more faint, and I could barely hear it now. Everyone else could still hear it, though. When they heard me speak, their first question was always to ask where I was from. Sierra Leone was a poor country. Most of the people were living in poverty. While our family was really well off due to my dad's involvement with the mines, what kind of money did he think I was going to make there?

I didn't want to be connected to the diamond mines at all. After all the corrupt forces mining there... blood diamonds and shit, that was the last place I wanted to be. I was fine right where I was. I was a thirty-two-year-old chemical engineer, making bank at Hargrove and Associates, Inc. I'd been working there for the past two years and had been able to save almost one hundred grand since then. Before that, I'd gotten my experience at one of the refineries in the area. I had plenty of money that my parents had sent me here with as well. "So, what's the woman's name that you're talking to?"

"Why does it matter, Jarius? It ain't yo' mama, so you shouldn't be worried about who I'm 'bout to slide up in."

"Nigga, fuck you. I was just asking. Get the fuck out of my chair."

I chuckled as I stood and looked in the mirror at my fresh lineup. He'd gotten my beard just right. Hopefully, tonight, Kyley would be running her fingers through it. Slapping a fifty-dollar bill in his hand, he slid it in his pocket and was about to call the next person to the chair. "Nigga, if you don't run me my ten dollars, I'm gon' sit back in yo' chair until I get it."

"Why you gotta be so tight?" He looked over at another barber and said, "Man, them Africans crazy when it come to their money."

He chuckled. Everybody was familiar with me in there and knew we joked around a lot. So, they didn't pay us any attention. He finally slapped my ten spot in my hand and I gave it back to him, as always. "You know this shit is stupid, right? You do the same shit every week."

"I don't want you getting comfortable with not bringing me my change. One day, I might need that shit."

He rolled his eyes, then we slapped hands and I headed out. When I got to my Range Rover, I saw that pretty, black, porcelain doll again that came out of the beauty supply store earlier. She was so gorgeous. I usually went for lighter to medium-brown complexioned women, but this woman made having a preference sound stupid as hell. I licked my lips as she walked back to the beauty supply store, looking at a bag of hair.

After cranking up, I decided to just leave. I was getting too old to still be sticking and moving. I was thinking about my future and my legacy a lot more these days than I wanted to. My one-nighters had slowed way down. The only way they were limited to one night now, was if the sex was trash. For the most part, I dipped back. The problem was that nobody seemed worthy enough to carry my name. Haji Okiro Abimbola. *Pilgrim born with fat cheeks and wealth.* While I didn't travel to America for religious purposes, it was definitely sacred compared to Sierra Leone. I was definitely born with fat cheeks and money, still had them both.

When I got home, I could only hope Kyley would be worth my time. She was pretty enough and had ass that could claim any man's attention. I met her at the post office earlier today when I went to mail some beard cream that Jarius sold in his barbershop to my boy. Glenn had moved back home to Austin after we finished school, but we kept in touch. When I left the line, I noticed her leaving her post office box. I couldn't help but holla at her. She'd smiled big when she looked at me and gladly gave me her number.

Hopefully, that wasn't a bad sign that she'd already called me, asking to come through. My dick hadn't been wet in a month, so I was way overdue. She was twenty-five and worked at Verizon while going to school to get her master's degree in family counseling. The more I thought about her, the more skeptical I was getting. What type of woman showed up at a nigga's house alone and at night the first day they met? She was that damn trusting? She was either a hoe or she was naïve as hell.

After grilling some chicken, I made a salad, while my old school southern rap playlist blasted through the speakers. "Let Me See It" by UGK was one of my all-time favorites. I danced a bit while I cut my vegetables and boiled eggs for my salad. All the memories I'd made at frat parties in my college years slid through my mind, making me smile. The ass that twerked on my dick after those parties... shiiid, I couldn't count. There were more Sigmas and Alphas on Lamar's campus back then, but me and my boys would ride out to Prairie View to party with the Q-Dawgs and the Kappas, getting ass in a three hundred mile radius. As I reminisced, my cell phone started ringing. Grabbing my remote to turn down the music, I grabbed my phone with the other hand. "Hello?"

"Kusheh, Haji! Aw di bodi?" my mom asked in Krio, my native language.

"Kusheh! Di bodi fayn! Aw di bodi?"

She squealed in excitement. She loved to hear me speak Krio. They swore I was so Americanized that I didn't remember it. I'd only roll my eyes. We spoke English in Sierra Leone. I didn't understand why they had to be over the top about everything, where I was concerned. She'd said, *hello, Haji! How are you?* And I'd responded, *I'm well.*

"Di bodi fayn!"

I chuckled. "How's everybody doing, Mama?"

"We're all fine, baby. I was about to turn in for the night and wanted to check on my baby boy."

They were five hours ahead of us here in Beaumont, so it was almost ten at night, there. "I'm glad everyone's good. I'm doing well, just preparing dinner."

"What are you eating?"

"Just a grilled chicken salad."

"Still sounds good. Your dad has a doctor's appointment in the morning, so I better get my rest. He's like a big baby when he goes to the doctor."

I chuckled. My dad rarely called me. He'd hear all about how I was doing from my mother and vice versa. She was our middleman unless he just couldn't avoid calling me. It was sad, really. He refused to talk to me because of decisions I made for my life. I didn't understand him sometimes. We loved one another and we both knew that, but it would be nice to hear him say it sometimes.

He was more concerned with appearances. The fact that I wasn't married yet had bothered him more than me living in America. I was at the age where I should have had a wife and children by now. Instead, I was too busy sowing my oats all over the country. His words, not mine. I was sowing them, but only in southeast Texas and southwestern Louisiana. "Okay. I hope all goes well. Talk to you soon."

"Okay, son. I love you."

"I love you, too, Ma."

I ended the call, then cranked my music back up and sat at the table with my salad and bottled water. I'd pour me a glass of Patrón later, before Kyley got here. If she wanted to get down, I wasn't gon' stop the show and it was always better when I had liquor in my system. As I ate, I received a text message. *I'm on my way.*

Looking at the time on my phone, it was only a little after five. She sure in the hell was coming early. I told her I should be home by five and she barely waited ten minutes past that. Whatever. I was just grateful I was off this weekend. I didn't feel like analyzing chemicals and samples. I was tired as hell because we were shorthanded. Companies expected their certificates of authenticity, what we called C of A's, in a decent amount of time. Those certificates told them what all was in the chemical sample they'd sent us. Being shorthanded made it even harder to get those out in a decent amount of time when we were busy.

Once I'd finished eating and had cleaned the kitchen, I poured a glass of Patrón and changed the playlist. It was my chill mix. Dwele hit the speakers, causing me to do as the song suggested and dim the lights. I sat on the couch and put my feet up on the ottoman, and surprisingly, my mind went back to that pretty, black doll going in the hair store. She was on my mind heavy, so I knew I would have to say *something* to her if I saw her again. She had a gorgeous shape, proportionate in every way and it commanded my attention. Her looks were perfect, but I wondered what her mind was like.

With all the women's legs I'd spread, I still hadn't found one that intrigued me intellectually. It wasn't that I was just so damn smart or had intelligent conversation *all* the time, but it would be nice to meet a woman that thought beyond the present... one that had shit in motion for their future. I was tired of that lackadaisical attitude, where they were just trying to land a nigga with money. However, I'd probably missed my one a long time ago, because of my reputation. She probably looked at me and said, *Damn, he fine as hell, but shit... he fuck everything with a pussy.* I had to shake my head at the thought.

Before my thoughts could get carried away in my mind, the doorbell rang. I gulped the Patrón and went to the front door. When I opened it, Kyley was standing there in a jumpsuit that looked like it had been painted on. I stepped aside and let her walk inside. "You have a nice house."

"Thank you. You want a tour?"

"Mmm-hmm. Let's end the tour with the bedroom."

Just what I thought. I should've hollered at Pretty Black earlier. This shit would probably be a one-night thing.

 hinara

"I'm sorry to tell you, but we have to lay you off."

"What? When?"

"Today is your last day, Chinara. I'm so sorry. We had to make some cuts, and three of you just started within the past year. We just aren't pulling the money in like we thought we would."

They always called me by my first name because they couldn't pronounce my last name, Nwachuku. They couldn't seem to grasp the fact that the N was silent. "I understand," I said as I turned to walk out.

Going to my desk, I started gathering my things. I didn't have much on my desk, because most of my time was spent in the DJ booth. I left my job at the news station to come here, thinking there were more opportunities here. I wanted people to hear my voice. The news station was ideal as well because I wanted to give little Black girls positive images of dark-skinned women making strides in society.

For as long as I lived here in Beaumont, I'd never seen a woman as dark as me as an anchor on the news. Sure, there had been some pretty, brown women to grace the TV screen, but again, none as dark as me. However, the news station only had me running errands and so forth. So, I came here in hopes of getting my voice and name out there first, then go back to a news station to apply for a job as an anchor. Apparently, that was the wrong choice.

I only had enough money to survive for a month on my own. My parents had allowed me to come here, knowing we didn't have the money for me to go back and forth to visit. Nigeria wasn't a hop, skip and a jump away. I'd never been able to afford a trip back home to visit since I'd come here ten years ago. Their security was the fact that my aunt lived here. That blanket was snatched from under me when she passed away two years ago from a major car wreck. I promised my parents and myself that I would make it on my own. I was living in her condo, but I knew I wouldn't be able to keep up the rent without having a job.

Once I gathered my things, I headed out to the parking lot. One of the DJs ran out to catch up with me. "Chinara, wait!"

Stopping, I took a deep breath as Donovan caught up with me. I was doing my best not to cry and worry about what I would do. Tomorrow morning, I would hit the ground running. Had I known this would happen, I wouldn't have made a hair appointment for this evening. I could have done my hair myself, but I wanted something cute and protective, so I'd gone to the hair store, as instructed, to get hair for my braids. "I'm so sorry. I really hate to lose you, but you are meant for greater. Use this opportunity to seek out greater."

"Those are encouraging words, Donovan, except that no one's hiring. I've been looking. Right now, I'll have to take whatever I can find, whether it's in communications or not."

I continued to my car that I would no longer be able to afford after the next monthly note. Calling my parents was out of the question. There was nothing they would be able to do to help. Times had only gotten harder on them and I was sending them money whenever I had extra. After I put my things in the backseat and closed the door, Donovan was still standing there. "I'm sorry, Chinara. I'll be looking out for you, too. Okay?"

"Okay."

Before I could object, he pulled me in his arms and hugged me. Ugh. He was always a little musty and it made my stomach turn. I didn't understand how he couldn't smell himself. When I pulled away, I adjusted my nose ring. I normally only wore a stud, but today, I'd decided to wear a loop. Donovan had my face mushed right into his chest. God, help us all. "Thank you, Donovan."

He opened my car door and I slid into the driver's seat. I cranked up my Avalon as he closed the door, then stared at myself in the rear-view mirror for a moment. It was facing me since I'd applied my lipstick before going into the building. Deciding to do the right thing, I called and canceled my hair appointment and just paid the twenty-five-dollar cancellation fee. That was a lot better than spending over two hundred dollars to get my hair braided.

Heading to the hair store, I decided to bring all that hair back for a refund and just get me some good moisturizers and maybe a cute wig. Turning the radio up, I tried my best to groove to the sounds of Lucky Daye. Huffing loudly, I knew I would soon lose that, too. Satellite radio wasn't a necessity. I pulled in the parking lot, and the moment I got out, my eyes met another pair, staring at me from the barbershop. *Oh my.* Brother must have been fresh out the chair. His beard was lined perfectly.

Making my way to the hair store, which was in the same strip, I noticed him taking slow strides in my direction. Today wasn't the day. I was in a funk and I wasn't about to tell some stranger all my business, making me look desperate for help. Nothing was worse than having a man thinking they were rescuing me. I found that out the hard way when I first got to America and couldn't afford those expensive-ass books. He'd bought my books with his financial aid refund, but he held that shit over my head the entire semester and tried demanding that I pay him back in other ways. Didn't happen, and eventually, he left me alone, thankfully.

The closer this guy got to me, the more handsome he appeared, especially when he smiled. *Dear God, why now?* "How you doing, Pretty Black Doll?"

I frowned slightly but decided to just accept the compliment. Plus, I heard a slight accent that definitely reminded me of my homeland. Being that it had sort of a British flavor to it, I knew immediately he was from Sierra Leone, or at least near it. "I'm fine. How are you?"

His eyebrows had risen slightly, and I knew it was in response to my voice and probably that I had an accent, too. I'd been told that my voice was sexy and could definitely put an angel's voice to shame. It was medium-ranged in pitch, but it was soulfully heavy. "I'm good now," he said, grabbing my hand.

I rolled my eyes and he chuckled. "My name is Haji and I wanted to know if it was possible to talk to you for a moment. I noticed you around here a couple of weeks ago, but I didn't approach you. So, I could only pray for another opportunity."

He had the tell-tale signs of a playa, and I didn't have the time, energy, nor desire to deal with someone like him. I supposed I was judging him slightly, but whatever. "Nice to meet you, Haji. I'm Chinara. I hate that you wasted your prayer time on me. Have a good day."

I slid my hand from his and went inside the hair store. Glancing back at him, he was still standing there with his bottom lip tucked in his mouth. He was so sexy, but oh well. I rolled my eyes again and went to the register, only to find out that I couldn't return the hair. It had been too long. I huffed, then walked out of the store to find him still standing there. Glancing at him as he clasped his hands together, giving me one of those looks that said he could fuck my world up, I continued to my car.

By the time I got there, he was approaching me yet again. His swag was undeniable, and I could tell that he'd been in the States just as long as I had, if not longer. Before he opened his mouth, I would have never guessed he was African. His attire didn't scream home. I wore African print sometimes, and I did my best not to indulge in much of the American culture when I first got here, but the food was my downfall. "Pretty Black Doll, can I have a minute?"

"My name is Chinara. I told you that already," I said as I spun around to look at him.

"My bad, African Queen. Let me start over."

"Kusheh. Mi nem na Haji. Ah gladi fo mit yu."

"So, you think speaking Krio is going to impress me, Mr. Salone?"

Back home we referred to Sierra Leone as Salone, combining it into one word. "I don't fluently speak the dialect, but I do know that you said hello, stated your name, and said nice to meet you. Now if you're done, I'm gonna go."

He frowned slightly. "You this hard all the time?"

"Look. I'm not in the best mood and I wish you would just... leave me alone."

He lifted his hands in surrender, although I could feel my middle pulsating. He turned me on, and I wasn't ready for that. "I'll let you be, Ms. Chinara. I just thought that maybe I could help lighten your mood. Sorry, I bothered you. A de go."

I took a deep breath and got in my car as he walked away, wishing he would have tried harder. I was stressed, and my normally friendly personality was nowhere to be found. *He tried, Nara.* Glancing back at him, he was standing on the sidewalk with his friend, but his eyes were on me. Cranking my car, I headed home, escaping the seriousness of his gaze. That didn't help his large frame escape my thoughts, though. He towered over me, so he had to be every bit of six-foot-three or taller. He was fine as hell, too. I could see his muscular frame beneath the shirt he wore. But his smile was everything and his dark chocolate skin made me thirsty.

By the time I got home, I realized he was all I thought about on my way here. Me losing my job or not being able to pay my bills had never crossed my mind. But there was also something about Haji that gave me pause. I didn't date somebody just to date them. I was twenty-eight and that phase of my life's journey was over. A committed relationship was high on my list of priorities. Bringing my things inside the condo, I sat them on the table, then flopped on the couch, bringing my hands to my face. The only person I could vent to about my problems was way in Nigeria. My sister, Daraja, had been my confidant, but whenever it came to my personal issues, she always went back and told my parents. They were the last ones I wanted to bother with my issues.

After getting up to put away my things and eating dinner, I decided to take a shower and call it a night. It was only seven, but I didn't feel like going anywhere. This weekend would find me in my house, searching for a job that paid relatively well. I was in hustle mode and I couldn't let anything deter me, including my growing interest in Haji.

aji

MAYBE I SHOULD HAVE MOVED BACK to Sierra Leone. I would have had time with my father. Maybe I could have gotten answers from him about our relationship. The same night that Chinara shut me down, my brother called me to say that my dad had fallen ill, and they weren't giving him much longer. Once I got here, he lived another two days, then passed away. He was no longer conscious, and no one seemed to know what had happened. He was doing fine one minute and the next, he'd collapsed on the floor, unresponsive.

My brothers seemed to be more torn up about his death than I was. I loved my dad, but I couldn't force the tears out if I tried. As I sat here in his recliner, I realized that our relationship may have been what kept me from properly grieving him. I somewhat resented him. It was like he couldn't just be happy for me. I was angry. And because of my anger, I had been in a nasty mood since I'd gotten here. No one wanted to be around me because I refused to speak Krio or to even hold friendly conversation. I'd been this way for almost two weeks.

Just being here in his house, knowing that he'd practically disowned me had me feeling a way. My mama was the only one that seemed to understand how I was feeling. As I sat there, I quickly got up and went outside. Thankfully, the sun had gone down. Sitting on the porch, I thought about Chinara... the pretty, black doll that shut my ass down. Thoughts of her seemed to be plaguing me since that very day. I'd never been shut down like that. She was so forceful and even though I was sincere in my attempt to get to know her, she wasn't hearing that shit.

I didn't know why in the fuck I was thinking about her rude ass anyway. My mama came and joined me outside. "Aw di bodi?"

I didn't wanna talk. "Haji, I know you're angry, but baby, I don't know what to say to make you feel better."

Exhaling, I turned to her and kissed her hand. She sat on the porch next to me and kissed my cheek. "Are you going to come to the reading of your father's will?"

"I don't know. I'm just ready to go home and get back to my life. I know you're suffering from his loss and I wish you would come to my place for a little while, but I know you won't. Y'all act like coming to America to visit me would be like going to hell. But it is what it is."

She lowered her head, then got up and went inside. Whatever the problem was, they wouldn't tell me, no matter how bad I tried to make them feel about it. My brother, Kevin, came outside and asked, "So, what did you do now? She's crying."

"Why it had to be that I did something? Man, get the fuck out my face."

He grabbed my shirt, trying to pull me from my seat, but he must have forgotten that he was the lil, big brother. I was almost twice his size. Standing to my feet, I pushed him away from me. "Kevin, you don't want this fight. You think Mama crying now, she gon' be screaming in a minute. If you wanna be buried next to your father, that's on you, but don't fucking touch me like that again or I'm gon' make that shit happen sooner than right now."

He was only two years older than me, but by the time I hit my last growth spurt when I was fifteen, I left him in my dust. Kevin was only about five-foot-eight but was always trying to manhandle me at six-foot-four and two hundred eighty pounds. Today would be his last time getting that reminder. "Why is my mother crying?"

"Because I told her the truth. I told her I wish she would come stay with me for a little while but her and your father act like I was asking them to come to hell to see me."

He shook his head. "You're so disrespectful. Her husband just died and, whether you like it or not... your father."

"You know what? I think I'm gonna go home. A de go na os," I said, giving him the satisfaction of repeating myself in Krio.

I walked in the house and stormed to the room I was staying in, throwing my shit in my suitcase. Afterwards, I sat on the bed and saw that the next flight to Houston wasn't available until tomorrow evening. *Fuck!* I booked it, then called for a ride to Mamba Point Hotel. As I made my way down the stairs, my oldest brother, Umaru, was waiting for me. "Haji, where are you going?"

"To a hotel. I can't be here any longer."

"Come to the reading tomorrow."

"My flight leaves out tomorrow. I don't even know why I'm still here. I'm the outcast of this family anyway. Y'all act like I'm committing sin by staying in America. I'm educated and well-established in my career. Where I choose to live should be of no consequence."

"Haji, the reading is at ten. What time is your flight?"

"Five."

"Please come. Dad left some things for us aside what he left for Mama. Hopefully, this can give you closure or insight into how he felt."

Umaru was always the voice of reason. He was seven years older than me and I always respected him growing up. He'd taught me and

Kevin a lot over the years. "Come pick me up in the morning," I said as I saw my car arrive.

He nodded as I walked past him, glancing into the kitchen to see my mother on the phone, sitting at the kitchen table, no doubt, telling the rest of the family how disrespectful I'd been. I thought she understood me and how I was feeling, but maybe I was wrong about that shit. When I walked outside, my cell phone rang. Seeing it was a call from Beaumont, I answered. It was probably Jarius calling from the barbershop. While it was almost dark here, I knew it was still afternoon there. "Hello?"

"How's everything, man?"

"Good. I'll be heading back tomorrow. My house still in one piece?" I asked as I got in the car that was here to transport me to the hotel.

"Nigga, yeah. You act like I been turning up in yo' shit. Well... I mean, I have, but I know how to clean up after myself."

"My house better be in the same condition it was in when I left. I ain't up for no bullshit when I get back."

"Man, chill out. I'll see you in three days. Enjoy time with your family. Oh! Shit, I almost didn't tell you. I saw yo' girl. She was going to the hair store. She glanced this direction like she was looking for you, too."

"Whatever. I ain't tripping over her ass no more. But we'll talk when I get back. Thanks, Jarius."

"No problem, bruh."

I ended the call just as we got to the hotel. Taking that two-day flight back wasn't something I was looking forward to so soon. Once I'd gone inside and gotten a room, I headed to the elevator, praying that tomorrow wouldn't prove to alienate me even more from the family.

WHEN WE WALKED into the attorney's office, something in me said I shouldn't have come. I didn't know why, but I was feeling like some bullshit was about to piss me off. There wasn't gonna be an understanding letter from my pops or soft words. He was a hard man, and I knew that even in death, he would still be a hard man. My mama had said that his insurance policy was for a couple of million, so maybe he was giving us a piece of that. What I didn't understand was why he didn't just leave it up to her how to divide it amongst us.

Ense was a hard man and there weren't many people he trusted. However, I always thought my mama would be one of the people he did. But whatever. I was just ready to sit and get this over with before I had to fuck Kevin up. He was looking at me like I wasn't supposed to be there. I didn't have a restful sleep, so I was already on edge. Umaru and his wife had picked me up and everything was cool until I got here. I could feel the anger inside of me trying to surface and it wouldn't take much more to have it pouring out of me.

I sat next to Umaru and Kevin and Mama sat on the other side of the table. When the attorney joined us, he greeted us all and got right to it. "Hello, Abimbola family. Ense left a wealth of things for you all. Money he'd set aside just in case something ever happened to him. He was always worried that being connected to the mines would find him dead somewhere, and as soon as the autopsy results are in, we will know exactly what happened. So, Afiong, the insurance policy is all yours and everything that's in your account. He set something aside for his sons."

We all looked at one another as my mama nodded in acceptance. I was curious as to how she felt about having control of the money and what was done with it now that he was gone. She was like his child, too. She only did what he wanted her to do. The attorney turned his attention to Umaru, and said, "Your dad set aside three million dollars to be split evenly between the three of you. Umaru and Kevin, you two will leave here today with cashier's checks. Which one of you is Haji?"

No one answered him, but because I was the only one staring at him, he knew which one I was. I *knew* some shit was about to go down. I should have had brunch by myself and brought my ass to the airport. He cleared his throat and said, "Umm... Mr. Abimbola has stipulations on your money. He's allowing you to take fifty thousand today, but the rest you can't have until you're married. And you have to be married for six months before you can get it."

My mama gasped as Kevin smirked and I could feel the tension in Umaru. "See. Even in death, he's still fucking with me. And none of you at this table think anything's wrong that. Keep the fucking money. All that shit."

"Haji, he's releasing the fifty thousand. Please, take it," my mama begged.

I snatched the envelope from the attorney's outstretched hand and stood from the table. "Haji, wait. There's more," the attorney said.

I knew none of that shit probably included me, and all it was going to do was make me angrier, but I sat. This would show them just how much he hated that I was doing my own thing, living my life for me. The attorney went on to divide properties, bonds, and jewels that he'd stashed away in safety deposit boxes, but my mother's eyes stayed on mine because, just as I thought, there was nothing else for me... at least I thought. "Haji, there is a letter here for you. It's from your father and it's personal, so if you don't want me to read it, I won't."

"Read it," I said nonchalantly as I leaned back in my chair.

This should be good. I could feel Umaru's spirit. He was trying to calm me down, but that shit wasn't working. Kevin still had that smug look on his face and Mama was the only reason I hadn't gone upside his head. When I left Freetown today, I wouldn't be back for a long-ass time, if at all. Staring at the attorney, he once again cleared his throat, like he was nervous. He began reading. "Haji. You've always been the son who chose to go against the grain. You wanted to do things on your own terms. What I realized about that, was that you are just like me. That's why we can't get along and that's why

I'm so hard on you. I don't want you to make the same mistakes I did."

I rolled my eyes and took a deep breath. We were nothing alike. I wasn't nearly as hard and emotionless as he was. The attorney continued. "You need to learn a valuable lesson in life. It's not about how many women you can conquer, but it's about having that one that will be your queen and stand beside you. A woman like your mother. I bought you property in Houston, Texas. It's a massive compound. I'm sure you can find a job there as a chemical engineer. But again, you have to be married for six months before you can get it. It's already furnished, and your portion of jewels is stashed away in a safe deposit box. The directions on where the box is located is attached to this letter, along with the property's address. The attorney will keep the keys until you have met the requirements."

It was all about control for him. For me to do what the fuck he wanted me to do. The attorney had stopped reading, so I asked, "You done?"

He shook his head rapidly, then continued, "My past is what killed my parents. I didn't want to listen. Trying to supply this white devil in New York with diamonds was hard. He was wanting them at a quicker rate than we could supply, so I started cheating my way through to get to that money. It cost me. All the money in the world can't bring my parents back. Although I have all this wealth to split between you all, it means nothing to me. I took my anger out on a country instead of an individual. That's why I didn't want you to stay there. But have it your way."

I sat up and looked at the lawyer as he folded the letter. "So, no apology, nothing saying how he was proud of me for my accomplishments... nothing."

He shook his head, then I looked around the table. "Y'all see? No matter how much I've accomplished, I was never good enough for him. I have two degrees and make six-figures a year without being underhanded or doing anything illegal, but that means nothing to him. He controlled all of you and because he couldn't control me, I was the outcast… the one who went against him. He can keep all that material shit."

I stood from my seat and walked out of the room, calling a car to come get me. Umaru joined me in the foyer. "I'm sorry, brother. For what it's worth, I'm proud of you."

"Thanks," I mumbled as he walked out to open his vehicle for me to get my luggage.

Just as I'd figured, I felt worse about staying for this reading. The material shit didn't mean a thing to me if I didn't have his approval for my accomplishments. I didn't waste his money. Neither of my brothers had furthered their education. They did okay for themselves, but I never made either of them feel less than because they depended on him to help them when they needed him. After graduating and getting a job, I didn't ask him for a dime. Most of the money he'd given me for school was still in my savings account.

I'd gotten plenty of grants that he didn't know about, simply because I was a foreign student, not to mention the part-time job I'd obtained. But when I got my citizenship, he could have died then… eight years ago.

I sat outside on a bench with my luggage as Umaru stood there with me. Neither of us had said a word. When Mama and Kevin walked outside, along with his and Umaru's wives, I stood. Pulling my mama to me, I hugged her, then let her go and sat back on the bench.

No words were spoken for a few moments. Then she said, "I love you, Haji. I know your dad loved you, too."

"He had a terrible way of showing that shit."

"I know. And for that I'm sorry. A bayg padin."

Glancing at her as my car arrived, I stood and grabbed my bags. After walking away and loading them in the trunk of the car, I turned back to my family, who were all just watching me. My last moment with all of them in Freetown, Sierra Leone, I said, "A de go."

That meant goodbye. There was nothing further to say. Getting in the car, he drove away, taking me to the airport five hours early.

4

hinara

NOBODY WAS HIRING. I was overqualified for fast food places, but the jobs I was qualified for weren't hiring. I didn't know what to do next. The rent was due next week, and I didn't have the money. It had been a month since I'd gotten fired and the money I had saved had kept me afloat. But that was all gone now. The state had issued me food benefits and I had a little unemployment money coming in, but it wasn't enough. My car was in my name, so I wanted to preserve my credit. I paid it and I only had enough money left to pay my phone bill and get gas.

I'd cried for nights on end because I just didn't know what would happen. In less than a month, I could be homeless... living in my car, praying for a miracle. My hair was a mess underneath my head wrap, and if I could, I would just go back home... to Nigeria. It took everything out of me when I called home and had to pretend that everything was okay. My mother had so many health issues already, I knew the added stress of worrying about me would kill her.

Going to the refrigerator, I realized I was in desperate need of a trip to the grocery store. Huffing loudly, I knew I didn't have much money left on the card. They only allowed me two hundred dollars a month. After buying four packs of meat and other food, that left me at the bottom of the barrel. Plus, I really didn't know how to budget. I never had to do that in the grocery store. It was the end of the month and I wasn't sure how much was left on the card. Getting dressed, I made my way downstairs and got in my car.

I had a few dollars in my bank account, but I would need that for gas. Calling the eight hundred number to get my balance, my heart sank when it said I only had fifteen dollars and eleven cents. That would have to last a week. I rested my head on the steering wheel, taking deep breaths. I would have to survive on the bare minimum. The problem was that I found myself eating a lot more, because I was home most of the day. Gathering my composure, I took off for the grocery store.

After calculating my cost to the tee, or so I thought, I headed to the cashier. I'd gotten a small roll of ground beef, noodles, and sauce to make spaghetti and a half-gallon of milk for the remaining cereal I had. It felt like I was sweating, trying to make sure I didn't go over. That didn't stop me from grabbing a pack of gum. Gum helped me control my eating. If I was chewing gum, I didn't think about eating so much. Loading the conveyor belt, I was cool until I saw him. *Haji.*

Shit! I hoped he didn't see me, but that was in vain because he was coming my way with a slight smile on his face. When he made it to me, the cashier had begun scanning my items. "Hey, pretty, black doll. Oh... a bayg padin... Hello, Chinara."

I rolled my eyes, but said, "Hello."

He put his shrimp, crabs, and other seafood items on the belt and my stomach growled. I wanted to crawl under the damn store when that happened. He chuckled and said, "I'm boiling all this today for me and a couple of friends. You ought to come by."

"No, thank you."

My face was so damn hot. Thankfully, I was pretty black because my face would have been red. "Your total is sixteen dollars and ten cents."

I frowned, but quickly scanned my card, knowing that it wasn't going to go through. I could see him watching me. The amusement on his face was now gone and he looked serious. He'd seen the card. *Ugh.* "Ma'am, you only have fifteen dollars and eleven cents."

"Okay. Take off the gum," I said softly.

"Use what she has available and I got the rest," Haji said from behind me.

It was only a dollar, but I felt horrible about it. "I have a dollar. I can pay for it myself."

"Quit being stubborn. It's a dollar."

I huffed and said, "Thank you."

Grabbing my things, I was about to head out when he said, "Chinara."

His voice commanded me to stop. It wasn't the playful, flirty tone I'd heard before. The seriousness of it took control of me. After paying for his things, he made his way to me. "Take my number."

"That's what you stopped me for?"

"Listen. I saw the card you used. I'm just trying to help you. You gotta be in a bad spot if you can't afford gum, Pretty Black."

"No. I don't need your help," I said, then walked away.

I couldn't make the same mistake twice. Letting a man help me, pretending to care about my well-being only to throw it in my face later was something I never wanted to experience again. Before I could get to my car, he grabbed my arm. "If you wanna suffer, go right ahead. I was offering to help out of the kindness of my heart and my genuine interest for you. Something told me when I saw you to go the opposite direction, and now, I know why."

He let me go and walked to his Range Rover. I felt horrible, but I didn't understand why. Haji was after something more than just helping me through a tough time. He was after my goodies. I could tell by the way his eyes caressed my body, making it heat up with desire... desire to feel his lips on every part of it. Shaking my head to rid myself of those illicit thoughts, I put my bags on the floor behind my driver's seat and got in the car. Glancing back in his direction, I saw him crank up his vehicle and take off.

He seemed angry, but what did I care? My life was none of his business. Men were hard to trust. They always seemed to have a hidden agenda. I hadn't had sex in nearly five years, and I was okay with that. I still had my self-respect, and that was what mattered most. Cheap thrills weren't something I was interested in. They needed to move my mind first, then my heart. My body would open up to a man in ways it never had. I'd been in love a couple of times, but obviously, it was only to teach me a life lesson.

Loving the wrong man only led to heartbreak. Although the first time I was in love, I was just a teenager in Nigeria, it still taught me a valuable lesson and that was to pay attention to the flashing red lights... signs that said something was off. Kemweh had taken my heart and slapped that shit around like it was a hockey puck. I was so young and naïve, I believed all his lies and excuses for not being what I needed. He was rarely present when I needed him to be unless I was offering something worth his while. He took my virginity like it was nothing to hold in high regard. And for a year... almost two, I gave of myself, my love, my heart, and way too many of my thoughts.

When I got home and got inside, I flopped on the couch. That seafood looked so damn good. I should have taken him up on his offer, but I couldn't imagine just going to his house. I didn't know him and, for all I knew, he could have done something horrible to me there. Knowing I needed to cook before my stomach fought me, I turned on the TV only to be met with a message saying that they'd turned off the cable and how to pay the bill. There went that. I turned the TV off and began cooking, hoping that the food would last for a week.

As I browned the ground meat, my cell phone started to ring, so I ran to it. Anyone could be calling for a job interview. It was an unknown number. "Hello?"

"Hello. May I speak to Chi-nara N-watchie-ku?"

I rolled my eyes slightly. "Hi. This is Chinara Why-choo´-koo," I said, enunciating the syllables of my last name.

"My apologies. My name is Kyley and I'm calling from Verizon. I wanted to see if you were still interested in the sales associate position."

"Yes, ma'am, I am."

"Great! Can you come in tomorrow morning for an interview?"

"Sure! What time?"

"Is ten o'clock good?"

"Yes, ma'am."

"Great. Just come to our location on Dowlen Rd."

"Okay. See you tomorrow."

I ended the call and did a dance around the front room. I was so damn excited, I forgot about the ground meat. "Nooooo!!!!" I screamed.

Smoke was coming from the kitchen as I ran in there. I'd burned the ground meat. After getting the pot off the fire, I sat it in the sink and ran water on it. The tears sprang from my eyes. This meal was supposed to last for five days until I got my benefits. I had to resort to eating cereal and milk. I didn't know what tomorrow was gonna bring, but I couldn't focus on it. All I could worry about was today and I was good for now. I'd have to worry about tomorrow once it got here.

I SAT on a bench in the lobby area, anxiously awaiting my turn to interview. There was another lady still inside. Bouncing my leg, I smoothed down my hair and decided to check my lipstick as I waited. I'd arrived ten minutes early, so someone had to open the door for me. This wouldn't be my first time working in a place like this... I meant retail. I'd worked at Wal-Mart before, but I didn't want to be stuck with working crazy hours.

The young lady finally emerged with a smile and she was quite chummy with the interviewer. That did absolutely nothing for my confidence. However, I took a deep breath as the young woman said, "Are you Chinara... umm..."

"Nwachuku?"

"Yes. I'm sorry."

"No problem."

"Come on in."

She was a young Black woman, with hair hanging down her back. She looked my age, maybe a couple of years younger. Offering me a seat, she asked, "So, where are you from?"

"I'm originally from Lagos, Nigeria, but I've been here for ten years."

"Oh. What brought you here? School?"

"Yes, ma'am."

"If you don't mind me saying so, honey... you're in the wrong industry."

I frowned slightly, not knowing where she was going with this. She looked over my resume for a moment, then said, "I was sure you'd been a model. You are gorgeous."

I chuckled out of embarrassment, then said, "Thank you."

I wished she would just hurry and get to the interview because I wanted to get back home before my stomach started to growl. Not eating breakfast was a mistake, but I was doing my best to preserve my food. She finally began asking questions about my degree and why I was wanting to work at Verizon. I did my best to make it seem like I wanted to work there. The truth was that I was desperate. I needed to work. I'd accept a job anywhere at this point.

Once she asked a few questions about my customer service experience, she smiled big and said, "It was so nice meeting you. I'm in awe of how genuine of a person you seem. Hopefully, I'll be in touch soon."

"Thank you. It was nice meeting you, too."

Not really. She seemed kind of fake to me. My people radar usually steered me right. She led me out to the lobby, told me to have a great day, and went back to her office as I made my way to the door. When I got to it, a man holding a bag was walking out of it and held the door open for me. My body nearly melted to the pavement when I looked into Haji's eyes. He only stared at me as he held the door. So I said, "Thank you, Haji."

His eyebrows lifted slightly, then he said, "You're welcome, Chinara."

I quickly walked away, making my way to my car, only to realize we were parked side by side. When he got to his expensive vehicle, he got in, but then got back out. Making his way around his car, he came to mine. Putting my window down, I stared into his dark eyes. "Everything in me is telling me to move on, but I have to try one more time. Can I take you to lunch? There are quite a few restaurants right here in the area we could go to."

Looking away for a moment, debating if I should answer him, I came to the conclusion that even if he took me to McDonald's, that was better than cereal and milk. I licked my lips and said, "Sure."

"Damn. For real?" he asked with a frown.

I smiled and he looked mesmerized. His gaze was serious, and it felt like he had the power to yank my soul from my body. "Yeah. For real. Lunch won't hurt nobody."

He leaned over against my car, then asked, "So, where do you wanna go? What do you like?"

I shrugged my shoulders slightly. I'd never really been to any of the restaurants because I didn't want to go alone. "Chick-fil-A is good."

He gave me a one-sided smile and said, "Man, just follow me."

He acted like I offended him by suggesting Chick-fil-A. That was doing something for me. They were definitely more expensive than McDonald's and Taco Bell. When he backed out, I followed him for a mile to Longhorn Steakhouse. My mouth watered at just the name of the restaurant. I hadn't had a steak in months. However, I wouldn't be inconsiderate and order pricey items from the menu. Then again, if he didn't take me up on going to Chick-fil-A, then he was telling me to get what I wanted.

As I grabbed my purse from the passenger seat and slid my phone inside, he'd opened my door. I smiled slightly and said, "Thanks."

He nodded, then led me to the door, opening it as well. Haji was making a great impression so far. He seemed to be a gentleman and I liked that. Once we were seated, he stared for a moment. I was hoping he would say something because he was making me uneasy. "So, what made you say yes?"

"I'm in a good mood today."

"What's different about today?"

I looked away and said, "Nothing really. Just woke up in a great mood."

"I guess I'll let you make it with that answer," he said, picking up his menu. "So where are you from?"

"Lagos, Nigeria. What part of Sierra Leone are you from?"

"Freetown."

I nodded, then looked at the menu. "You came here for school, I assume. What was your major?"

"I majored in chemical engineering. I been done with school for eight almost nine years now."

"Oh. I majored in communications. I've been here for ten years. Are you here permanently?"

"Yep. I'm a citizen."

I nodded as the waitress came to take our drink orders. We continued our conversation, getting to know one another while we waited for her to come back with our drinks. We discussed our ages and our time here in Beaumont, Texas. We briefly talked about our families, but I seemed to do most of the talking concerning that. Then came the dreaded question. "What were you doing at Verizon?"

"I umm... I had an interview."

He frowned slightly. "I thought you had a communications degree. Why you applying there?"

"No one is hiring. So, I had to leave my area of expertise if I wanted to find anything."

"Oh."

He didn't push for more answers, and thankfully, the waitress came back to take our orders. He ordered the biggest damn steak on the menu, so I knew I was cool with ordering what I wanted. Once she walked away, he resumed our conversation. "So, how long have you been searching for a job?"

Taking a deep breath, I exhaled slowly. He made me feel so comfortable, but I didn't feel as comfortable telling him this. But somehow, I managed to say, "I got laid off the same day you first tried to talk to me."

"That was like... over a month ago," he said with a slight frown.

"Yeah."

"So why you so proud, Pretty Black Doll? Let me help you."

"I don't know you. For all I know, you could think I owe you for this lunch."

He frowned even harder. I noticed that he frowned a lot. Way more than he smiled. Maybe it was something about me that was making him frown. "Everybody ain't out to sabotage or use you."

After that, the rest of the lunch was quiet. I knew I'd really offended him now. But what was I supposed to think? He didn't know me. Why was he being so nice? Wanting to get to know some-body and helping them financially were two totally different things. You didn't offer financial help to strangers unless you were going to benefit from the situation somehow. When the waitress brought out our food, I was grateful. My stomach had been growling the entire time, and I just wanted this awkward-ass moment to be over.

aji

CHINARA WAS ONE PROUD-ASS NIGERIAN. Sometimes, they were the most stubborn creatures on earth, afraid to admit that they needed help. I understood that she didn't know me, but shit. Who turned down a trip to the grocery store? She was sitting there starving. I could hear her stomach growling from where I sat. That was the only reason she came to lunch with me. Once I heard that shit, I had to let my puffed-up chest deflate. I thought I'd finally gotten to her, but it was those damn missed-meal cramps that had her smiling and accepting the lunch date offer.

She didn't eat all her food. Just because I came from a wealthy family, didn't mean I didn't know the tricks of the trade. Sierra Leone was one of the poorest countries on the continent. She was saving that shit for dinner. It wasn't that she was full. She needed to assure that she'd have something to eat later. I felt sorry for her, but I could tell I was making her uncomfortable, so I chilled on the questions.

The rest of the lunch was uncomfortable as hell. It was like, she'd completely shut down on me. When we got outside, I asked if I could have her number and she gave it to me hesitantly. After programming it in my phone, I lifted her hand, kissed the back of it and left. I almost followed her to her place just so I could get her groceries anyway and bring them to her, but I figured I'd leave the shit alone.

When I got home, I flopped on my couch, planning to watch a movie, but that shit ended up watching me. I didn't have to go back to work until Monday, because my original plan was to leave Freetown today. So besides working out in the mornings and hanging around the house, I didn't have shit to do. I woke up to my phone ringing. I noticed Kyley's number on the screen. Rolling my eyes slightly, I answered, "What's up?"

"Hey, Haji. I saw you in the store. You off today?"

"Yep."

I wondered if she saw me with Chinara. That was probably what this call was for. She was tryna feel me out without just coming out and asking. I was a smart dude and felt a lot of shit. These women thought they were being slick about their moves, but that shit was clear as hell to me. "Can I come through on my lunch break?"

"Why yo' lunch break and not when you get off?"

"I don't get off until seven and I'm going out with my girls. But I could use some dick to get me through the rest of the day."

"Come through, then."

"Alright. See you in an hour."

I ended the call. If the sex wasn't good, I would have curved the fuck out of her. She was fine as hell and I'd beat that shit out the frame if she wanted me to. It wasn't like I had any prospects. She wasn't the one, that was for sure. Since I accepted her request, she had to know my status hadn't changed, but she was also trying to stay fresh on my mind. I didn't want her ass, though... well, I wanted her ass but not her heart. For some reason, I believed she was cool with that, too.

After taking a shower to freshen up, I drank a shot of Patrón to level me out a lil bit, then turned the music on through the speakers of the house. Listening to SiR talk about fucking and leaving fit us perfectly. Kyley was a lil ratchet and I liked that shit. Which was why I was gonna bring her to my private room in the back of the house that I enjoyed entertainment in from time to time. There was a stripper pole in there. I needed to see what she was working with.

Pretty Black Doll entered my mind again, but I knew I needed to quit pining over her. That wasn't my style anyway. Something about her said queen status, though. It felt like she was the woman that would show me all the things I was missing out on by being single. But fuck it. I couldn't make her do some shit she didn't wanna do. I'd given her my number, too, so hopefully, she would eventually decide to use it. As I tried to push Chinara from my thoughts, my doorbell rang.

Walking to the door, I brought my glass to the kitchen, then went to the door to let her in. By the time I closed the door and turned around to her, she was already taking off her clothes. "Damn. You ready for this dick, huh?"

"Hell yeah."

"Follow me."

Elliott Trent was playing through the speakers, and when she saw the stripper pole, her ass didn't ask no questions. She went straight to it. That shit had me skeptical. I pulled my shirt off and pulled the condom out of my pocket. She dropped her clothes to the floor, then slowly pulled off her bra and underwear. She left her heels on and twirled around that pole like it was home... all comfortable-looking and shit. I frowned as I took my pants and boxers off and stroked my dick. Yeah, her ass was a pro. "Yo' ass comfortable up there."

"I take pole dancing classes. I've been waiting on an opportunity like this."

I sat in a chair in front of the small stage area and watched her handle business on that pole. The way she moved on that thing, she was a muthafucking lie. She was a damned stripper. Had to be. She danced her way to me and fell to her knees, taking my dick in her mouth quick as hell like it was melting, sucking my shit with plenty of suction. I grabbed a handful of her hair and jutted my hips forward, my dick at the back of her throat, producing plenty of saliva.

Releasing it, she licked her way to my balls, gently sucking and licking each one, then went back to the coveted prize. We ain't have all that time, so I opened the condom and pulled her off it. She wasn't the best at giving head anyway. Too much teeth involved. But that pussy, though, was another story. After sliding the condom on, I said, "Come sit on this shit."

"Can you hit it from the back instead?"

I rolled my eyes and stood from the chair, then brought her to the back of it, pushing her over it. I allowed my spit to drop down to her pussy, then massaged it in with my dick and pushed inside of her. Just from the initial thrust, she was screaming like I was killing her. I knew I had a big dick, but shit, she was tripping. This wasn't our first time and she didn't do all this shit then. I hadn't even gotten the shit all the way in. She was performing and that shit was a turn-off.

I could feel my dick getting soft, so I slapped her ass and said, "Man, shut the fuck up."

She turned to stare at me as I slammed into her. I pushed her head down, then picked her hips up to me to where she couldn't move. She had no choice but to take what the fuck I was giving her. Watching all that ass jiggle on my dick was just the motivation I needed to nut. "Ahh, fuck!" I growled.

Releasing her hips, I allowed my dick to slide out of her. When she turned around, she asked, "Shit, what's wrong with you?"

"Nothing, but all that extra shit you was doing was turning me off."

She nodded, then went to her phone to look at the time. "Well, thanks for the tune-up. I gotta go so I can get something to eat and get back to work."

After she was dressed, I walked her to the door and watched her walk out of it. She turned and said, "Bye, Haji. Until next time."

I gave her a head nod, then closed the door. I didn't even bother to respond to her. She'd probably never be back. I knew she was the one who'd interviewed Chinara at Verizon. If she got the job, they'd be able to discuss their much different adventures with Haji Abimbola. They were both in my past now.

Going back inside, I took another shower, washing and conditioning my beard this time. I'd been back home for a couple of days and I had yet to hear from anyone in my family. I wasn't surprised, though. Ever since I'd come to America, it was like I was shunned, but that was cool. I was doing well for myself and couldn't nobody take that from me. When I got out of the shower, I decided that I would order in for dinner. I didn't feel like cooking and my body was tired as hell. After putting my new screen protector and case on my phone, I cranked up some rap music and poured me a drink.

Once I sat on the couch, my phone rang, showing I had a call coming in from Jarius. I answered, "What's up?"

"Yo, man. I don't know what's going on with yo' pretty black doll, but I just seen her at the food bank."

I rolled my eyes because she was so damned stubborn. Jarius donated to the Southeast Texas Food Bank all the time. It was one of the things he did to give back to the community. "How you seen her?"

"Well, I ain't tryna push up on yo' crush or nothing... but she so fine, she sticks out in a crowd."

I exhaled loudly. "Man, don't be saying no shit like that. Grown men and crushes don't go in the same damn sentence. She lost her job a month ago and hadn't been able to find anything else, but her ass too stubborn and proud to accept help."

"How you know all that shit?"

"I took her to lunch today. When I went to Verizon, she was there interviewing for a job. She said yeah when I asked, but once we were there, I knew she used me for a free meal. I could hear her stomach growling the whole damn time."

"So, peep this... You oughta proposition her. She obviously in a bad way financially."

I frowned, trying to figure out what he was talking about. Then that shit hit me like a ton of bricks. "Ask her to marry me?"

"Hell yeah. You need a wife for six months and she need money. Sound like a win-win to me."

"Shiiiid, you ain't lying. Get my money, house, and jewels and chill the fuck out for a minute. But I already know her ass ain't gon' do it. She too proud, man. Plus, she seem like one of those morally sound women. She thanked me for lunch and burnt off. She barely kicked it with me long enough to get my number. I knew she ain't have nothing to go rush and do, but shit... she left a nigga like she was late for work."

"You never know unless you ask. All she can say is no."

"I'on know... she just different to me, man."

"Damn, you really feeling her. That has to be real shit."

"I know, but she ain't fucking with me. I might bring it up and see what she says the next time I see her. That's something I'd have to ask in person. I wouldn't be able to function with her in my house for six months. My dick gon' be pissed that I have all that beautiful, rich-looking chocolate in my reach and not give him a taste."

Jarius laughed loudly and I rolled my eyes. Chinara... shit, just thoughts of her was making my dick stand. It took everything in me not to say what I was thinking while we were out to lunch. I was normally a straight-forward guy, but something about her had me doing things differently. That shit was irritating me, too, because then I was left with all the thoughts of what I wanted to say to her. While I knew it was more than sexual, I wanted to dig up in her walls and make it a home. Those thoughts made me so damn sensitive to her. Everything in me wanted to say, *You on the verge of starving and you got the nerve to be proud?*

"Well, whatever, dude. You heard from that other chick you fucked with? I can't even remember her name."

"Kyley just left from here. That's probably gon' be my last go 'round with her ass. I think she saw me with Pretty Black today and now she tryna make sure she got a spot. She interviewed Chinara for the position at Verizon."

"Aww shit. That sounds messy as hell."

"Who you telling? I hope Chinara don't get the job. Kyley try to make people think she's more than what she is. She doesn't have the ability to hire Chinara. She can only recommend a second interview."

"Okay. One of two things can happen. One. She could be a hater and choose not to send Pretty Black through—"

"Naw, nigga. Pretty Black is my name for her. If you gon' use that name, make sure you say, *yo'* pretty black."

"Man, what-the-fuck-ever. She ain't yours. Anyway. Like I was saying. She could choose not to push her through, or she could be a messy bitch and push her through to get to you. You know, pump her for information, then God forbid, get close enough to her to tell her y'all fucking."

I had to get to Chinara and get her to accept that proposition. Because if Kyley got her hired, that would ruin all opportunities for me to get next to her. "Yeah, you right. Fuck! I'm gon' have to get to her and talk to her about it. I don't know how I'm gonna get her to accept it, though. Plus, that'll be my way of helping her at the same time and maybe getting close to her."

"Now you thinking on my level!" Jarius said, then chuckled.

"What level is that? Fuckboy status?"

"Nigga, say what the fuck you want, but that shit gon' get you what you want. It's playa shit and you know that. You don't have to be that way once you get her in your house."

"Whatever. I'll see you tomorrow for my weekly edge up."

"A'ight."

I sat there thinking, trying to figure out if that was the right move. But what other moves did I have? It wasn't like she was trying to hear me. I could tell she was feeling me, but she was fighting it because she didn't trust me. I didn't know how she was gon' get to that point if she didn't wanna kick it with a nigga.

After ordering my dinner, I chilled out, watching a basketball game. Holding my phone in my hand, I contemplated calling her, but something wouldn't let me do it. I was only going to offer to take her to dinner one day this weekend. Sitting my phone beside me, I huffed and rested the back of my head against the sofa cushions. Maybe I should just forget about the shit like I said I was gonna do. But that was a million in cash and possibly another couple of million in property and jewels. Did I wanna just let all that shit sit there? *Hell naw.*

 hinara

AFTER GETTING everything moved into a storage unit, I was tired as hell. I'd been evicted, but I knew that would happen. They gave me a month after the rent was due to get my shit together. I'd slowly been moving shit into a storage unit. Until I could find something else, I would have to live in my car. At least I didn't have to keep up with the utilities anymore. I'd be able to save a little money. After taking a shower, I turned the key in and quietly made my way to my car with a duffle bag, pillow, and blanket.

I'd never been this low, but I knew something would have to give. For now, I'd park at a truck stop and get some sleep. My ex-coworker, Donovan, had called a couple of times, but I couldn't bear to answer the phone. Haji had also called, but I declined his call as well. It seemed he could see right through me. No matter what I said, it was like he wanted to call out, *bullshit*. His eyes were so intense. He was so damn fine, too. I just couldn't understand why he was wanting to help me. What was his motive? It didn't matter, since I wasn't talking to him right now.

When I got to the truck stop, I crawled to the back seat and spread my blanket out. Thankfully, it wasn't hot outside. So, I could turn my engine off and still be comfortable. Just as I laid my head on the pillow, someone knocked on my window, scaring the shit out of me. When I sat up, he said, "I'm sorry, ma'am, but you can't sleep here unless you're in a big rig."

I nodded and let the couple of tears I had left drop down my cheeks, then climbed back in my front seat. I didn't know where to go. Glancing at my phone, I wanted to call Haji so badly. He was the only person I knew that would be willing to help me. But at what cost? What would he want in return? I was so desperate at this point, I was willing to go see if I could make money stripping. I hadn't heard from Verizon and it had been three weeks since my interview. I'd called a couple of times to check and they only said they were still interviewing.

I'd even called around checking all the other places I'd put in applications and submitted resumes to. No one wanted me. It had been two months since I'd lost my job and I just couldn't seem to come out on top. I was drowning. Leaving the parking lot, I decided to go back to the apartment complex and park in a different spot. Maybe I would go unnoticed.

Pulling around to the back side, opposite the dumpster, I quickly crawled to my back seat and got comfortable. This wasn't what I had in mind when I came to America to pursue my dreams of being in the business... being on TV. I just wanted to be successful. What was wrong with that? It was like this American soil refused to let me be great. If something didn't happen for me soon, I would be doing my best to get back home.

WHEN I WOKE UP, I went to the convenience store to brush my teeth and wash my face, then headed to the hair store. I needed more product for my hair to keep it looking healthy. I tried to go early, because both times Haji had seen me there, it had been in the evening. Looking at the mess of clothing in my front seat, I knew I'd have to do something about it. My car looked a mess. Just because I was sleeping in my car, it didn't have to look like it.

Once I got to the hair store, I quickly got the ORS product I used in my hair and headed back to my car. My damn heart stopped beating when I saw Haji standing there, waiting for me. He glanced in my backseat, then looked back at me. Quickly dropping my gaze to the ground, I continued walking to my car, knowing that I would have to explain. When I got to him, before I could open my mouth to say a word, he said, "Get in your car and follow me. Now."

I didn't dare say a word back to him. The anger that I saw in his eyes nearly paralyzed me where I stood. He walked away to his vehicle and I realized that he was here when I got here. He wasn't in his Range Rover. He was in a Benz. Getting in my car, my heart was beating rapidly, and I didn't know what to expect as I followed him out of the parking lot, on to Washington Boulevard. For the next fifteen minutes, I followed him, ending up at a beautiful, two-story home on Fir Lane.

I had never been on this side of Beaumont. I'd heard of Tram Road, which was the road we took to get here. I parked and just stared at it, wondering why he had me follow him here. When he opened the garage, I realized this was his home. Bringing my hand to my chest, I laid it flat, begging my heart to slow down. As I looked around, he motioned for me to pull in the garage. I shook my head no. I was wanting to back out the driveway altogether. Haji walked to my car and knocked on the window. As I put it down, he said, "Look. I'm tired of fighting with yo' ass. Pull the damn car in the garage, so I can show you where you will be living."

"I *cannot* stay here. What are you thinking?"

"That I ain't comfortable wit' yo' address being Toyota Avalon. You don't wanna stay here? Give me a better option."

I was quiet as he stared at me. Weighing my options, I put my window up and drove into the garage. *Nara, this is a blessing. Accept it as such.* I got out of the car and Haji was standing there with his hands in his pockets. "Why are you sleeping in your car? And don't lie to me."

Swallowing hard, I said, "I still haven't found a job and I couldn't afford the rent. I had to leave. My unemployment benefits aren't enough for me to be able to afford another place, not with my car note. This is so hard. I just wanna go home... to Lagos."

A tear slid down my cheek and he walked closer to me. Swiping the tear from my cheek, he said, "It doesn't have to be. Come on."

Grabbing my hand, he led me to the house. There was a beautiful pool in the back yard, and I could see that there were two rooms on the second story that had balconies. Once he opened the back door, I was in awe. Stepping inside, I was frozen in place. This house was amazing. "Haji... wow. This is a beautiful house."

"Thank you. Get used to it. I'm 'bout to take you on a tour and you can pick the room you'd like to sleep in. There's four of them... well, five total. I don't mind sharing mine," he said with a smirk.

I rolled my eyes and was about to say something before he cut me off. "Chill out Pretty, Black Doll. I'm just kidding... unless you *wanna* share. I ain't gon' object."

I exhaled loudly, then followed him around the massive house. The kitchen was to die for, and I could imagine cooking lots of meals in there. After showing me the dining area and the front room, he took me upstairs. "Here are the bedrooms. This one and the one next to it have bathrooms inside them, but the two with the balconies do not. You'd have to go to the hallway bath."

"Haji... thank you."

I allowed the tears of gratitude to fall down my cheeks. I still wondered if there would be anything that he would require of me. Living this lavishly had never been a reality for me. I was so over-

whelmed, that I could barely function. He walked closer to me and leaned in, kissing my forehead. "Let's go get your things out of your car and we'll go to lunch afterwards. There's something I need to talk to you about, too. Just have an open mind. Okay?"

Shit. I should have known there would be a catch to living here. Closing my eyes briefly, I responded, "Okay."

Vulnerability had taken over my life. I would do almost anything to not have to go back to sleeping in my car, especially now that I'd seen his home and knew just how relaxed this environment could be for me. Following him back outside, I got everything from the inside and popped my trunk so he could start getting my things from there. "Are you gonna sleep in one of the rooms with the bathroom?"

"Yes. Thank you. The one with the big window."

"Quit saying thank you. I'm very interested in you. Because of my interest, I'm willing to do what I can to help you. I wanna get to know more about you. That cool with you?"

I nodded shyly, then followed him back inside. When we got to the room I would be sleeping in, Haji opened the closet and I almost died. It was bigger than my room at the condo. "Oh my God! This closet is going to swallow my lil clothes!"

I laughed loudly, but Haji didn't crack a smile. "We gon' have to change that then."

He winked at me, then walked out, leaving me to myself with my thoughts. I threw myself to the bed, then wanted to stand and start jumping in it like a kid. I couldn't believe that I was here. Fate was something I believed in, though. It had to be fate for me to meet Haji and for him to be so persistent. God knew that I would need him... that I would need somebody to have my back during this time.

When he came back into the room, he had the rest of my things. I sat up and for the first time since he'd seen me, he smiled. Smiling back, I stood from the bed and began bringing my toiletries to the bathroom. I didn't have much. Haji came in with some of my hair stuff. "I left the towels in the trunk. You won't really need those. But

if you want, I can bring them in for you to put in one of the drawers in the closet."

"We can do that later."

He nodded, then continued to help me get my things situated. After getting everything put in the bathroom, we began hanging my clothes. "So, what made you want to become a chemical engineer?"

"I've always been good at math and science. After researching the area and I saw all the refineries, I decided on that because I knew I would be able to find a decent paying job in that industry. Why are you so hard? Why wouldn't you give me the time of day before?"

"I umm... I thought you were playing games. You seemed like a playa to me. That's the vibe I got, anyway. Being toyed with isn't on my to-do list. When I date, it will be with a purpose. One day, I wanna get married."

He nodded. "So, you said I *seemed* like a playa. I don't seem like one anymore?"

"Actually, yeah. You do."

He laughed and it made me laugh. His smile and laugh were so infectious. When he'd calmed down, he said, "Damn, baby. I used to be one, for real. The behavior left but the swag is still there. I ain't being celibate or no shit like that, but I don't be out searching for shit, either. But real shit, when I saw you, Pretty Black, I damn near lost all train of thought. You're beautiful and I plan to show you that I'm sincerely feeling you."

I was at a loss for words, so I nodded and continued to hang up clothes. When we were done, he led me out of the closet and closed the door. From what he was showing me, he was a sweetheart and I hated that I might have prejudged him based on my assumptions. Once we were downstairs and inside the kitchen, he turned to me. "You are free to do whatever in here, like it's your house, too... I mean, except bring another nigga in here. You haven't expressed a desire to get to know the nigga standing in front of you, so you may not be interested. I don't have a choice but be okay with that if that's the case, but if you choose to be with somebody else, you gon' have to go to his shit with that."

I shook my head slowly. I didn't wanna tell him whether I was interested or not, but I could already tell that he wasn't gonna make that easy for me. Catching me off-guard, he pulled me to him. Letting his eyes scan me from head to toe, he licked his lips. "So, what's up? You feeling a nigga or not?"

"I don't know yet. You seem cool to be around, though," I said softly.

He gave me a one-cheeked smile. "Just cool, huh? I got a lotta work to do, then."

As he gently pulled me to the door, I grabbed my purse from the countertop where I'd left it when we first got here. "So, where we going for lunch?"

"Chick-fil-A."

I laughed and clapped my hands, feeling super excited. He chuckled and I couldn't help but reach up and pinch his cheeks. They were so chubby. I was willing to bet he'd gotten that as a kid all the time. When I did, though, he stopped walking and stared at me. He knew I was feeling him, no matter what I said. "Chick-fil-A cannot be that damn good to you."

"But that's where you're wrong. That spicy chicken sandwich is everything. And the lemonade? It tastes like I licked the pearly gates of heaven."

"What the hell?" he asked, then laughed loudly. "I didn't realize you were so funny."

"I'm usually not, but someone rescued me from my own stubbornness and pride. That has me feeling so amazing. But it also has me wondering what I did to deserve such a blessing."

Choosing not to respond to me, he grabbed my hand and led me to his Benz. Opening the door for me, he held my hand until I'd sat, then closed the door. I'd never sat inside a Benz. *My God.* The seats were so plush. When he got in the car, he smiled at me. "I know we're just going to lunch, but do you know what you'd like for dinner? We can cook or we can go to dinner."

"Can I cook something for you as a thank you for taking me in?"

I slid my hand over his as I awaited his answer. "Pretty Black, it's taking everything I got in me to be a gentleman. I been wanting to kiss you since we first got here. I said that because if you touch me one more time, those pretty-ass lips gon' feel mine whether you ready for that or not."

Slowly pulling my hand away, I exhaled slowly. I'd admired his lips since day one. "I'm sorry," I said softly.

"You good. But yeah, you can cook. Tell me what you wanna cook so I know if we need to go to the store."

"You have rice? Beef meat? Vegetables?"

"I have rice. What type of beef meat?"

"Stew meat."

"It's frozen, so it might be best to just go to the store."

I nodded. After getting to Chick-fil-A, Haji opened my door and held my hand all the way to the entrance. Once we'd ordered our food, we sat in a booth to wait for our order to come out. At that moment, I remembered that he said he wanted to talk to me. "So, what did you wanna talk about, Haji?"

He shifted in his seat, then looked up at me. "I wanted to know if you'd marry me."

aji

"Na what na? You couldn't have said what I think you just said. No, I imagined it. I'm tripping. What did you say?"

I smiled slightly. "I wanted to know if you would marry me."

"Umm, is this a joke? I feel like I'm being filmed for some kind of show like Punk'd or something. You can't be serious."

"When my dad died, he left a will to be read to the family. He left his three sons a million dollars each, property, and jewels, but I was the only one who had a stipulation placed on getting my inheritance. I have to be married and stay married for six months. I'm asking you to marry me, but you'll be free to come and go as you please. While I really am feeling you, I'm not sure that I'm ready to marry anybody, for real. After about seven or eight months, we can get it annulled. In return, I will take care of you financially and when I get my money, I'll give you a hundred grand."

She lowered her head to her hands and mumbled. Lifting her

head, she shook it slowly. "I knew there had to be a catch to your generosity. Nothing is ever free, and niggas don't just do shit out of the kindness of their hearts anymore. I should have known better."

Taking a deep breath, she again slid her hand down her face. The young lady brought our food to us and took the plastic number sitting on the table. Once she walked away, she said, "So what happens if I say no?"

"Nothing. You can still stay at my place as long as you need to, and I'll still be interested in getting to know you... pursue something meaningful with you. I'll just be able to get what's mine a little sooner if you say yes. My pops never liked the fact that I wanted to come to America or that I was screwing around my first few years here. He hated that I stayed after finishing school. So, he put those stipulations on me getting my money. Please, Pretty Black?"

"Let me think about that. I don't know. Shit! This is a lot to think about, Haji. Getting married isn't something I take lightly. How long do I have to decide?"

"As long as you need. I'm sorry that I made lunch awkward, but I needed to see what you would say. Just the fact that you have to think about it got me all excited. You could have said no. You wouldn't have to work or do anything... just live in peace, baby."

She know she could use the money. It would be in her best interest to take the deal. "So, you saying I would be your legal concubine. What about umm... uh... will I have to have sex with you?"

"At least once to consummate the marriage," I said with a smirk.

"You full of shit. Consummate a fake marriage?"

"Well, you asked."

I chuckled as we ate. I could admit that this was a lot to think about for her. However, for me, it was simple. If she started feeling more for me, we could stay married. She was the woman I wanted, and I felt that shit in my bones. When she'd put her hands to my face and pinched my cheeks, I wanted to snatch her ass up then. "What stipulations are there?"

"We have to go out every now and then... you know, be seen

together like now... somewhat affectionate like we were earlier. That's about it. It has to be believable."

She took a bite of her chicken sandwich and she didn't say shit else while we ate. I knew I shouldn't have said shit about her marrying me. I let Jarius pump my ass up about this and I felt weird as hell. I was gonna call and cuss his ass out when I had time alone.

Once we'd finished eating, we headed to the store to pick up a few items, then headed home. Having Chinara in my home was surreal. I'd been fiending for her touch and now that I could possibly get it, I jumped the gun by asking her so soon. Had I let her get more comfortable, she probably wouldn't have felt like a fish out of water.

After walking inside, I retreated to the bonus room above the garage to shoot some pool. I needed to think. I probably should have waited to ask her that. *Shit!* Pulling out my phone, I called Jarius. He answered on the first ring. "What's up?"

"I might have scared her off listening to yo' ass."

"What the hell you talkin' 'bout?"

"I asked Chinara to marry me earlier."

"Nigga, already?"

"Yeah. She didn't totally shoot me down, though. So, it's possible she could still say yes, but I shouldn't have let yo' ass talk me into that shit to begin with. It sound so fuckboy-ish. How am I gon' convince her that I really do have feelings for her with this looming over us?"

"Quit tripping, man. Let whatever gon' happen, happen. Pretty Black gon' be down. I think she prolly feeling you, too. Whether she wanna admit that shit or not. Once she thinks about the shit, she gon' see that it's a win-win situation. I got a head I'm cutting, so let me know what she say."

"A'ight, man. And remember to watch yo' damn mouth. She's *my* pretty black."

"Aww nigga, shit."

He ended the call. I was tripping. I was way more worried than I should have been. She didn't say no. So, it probably wouldn't be any hard feelings even if she did. Turning on the music from my phone, I went poured me a glass of Henny. My nerves were still shot because I was anticipating what she would say. She could decide to not give me her answer for months. As I sipped my drink, she came back down the hallway into the room. Walking closer to me, she lowered her head and said, "I'll do it."

Damn! I didn't expect her to make a decision *this* quick. Setting my drink down, I stepped even closer to her and grabbed her hands. "You sure?"

"Yeah, but I need to set some boundaries of my own."

"A'ight. You want a drink?"

"Please. Whatever you're having."

I poured her some Henny in a cup and handed it to her, then gestured for her to follow me to the couch. We both sat and she angled her body toward mine as I tipped my cup back, killing the liquid inside. I scooted closer to her as I sat the cup on the coffee table. Grabbing her hand, I held it between mine and tucked my bottom lip in my mouth, waiting for what she had to say. After staring at me for a moment, she quickly downed her drink as well. *Yeah, she wanted me just like I wanted her ass.* I didn't know why she was playing games.

She sat her glass next to mine, then looked at me. "When we're here, that doesn't give you the freedom to do what you want with my body. I give the greenlight for any... activities. And that's *if* any activities are explored."

Scooting closer to her, I could see the goosebumps on her skin. I stared at her lips for a moment, then licked my lips and leaned in, softly kissing her lips. Maintaining my position after taking my lips from hers, I asked against her lips, "Activity like this?"

Her nipples were straining against her blouse as I lightly slid my fingertips down her leg. My eyes were trained on those imprints. I wanted nothing more than to take all her shit off right now and please her body beyond her wildest desires. "Activity just like this, Haji. I didn't give the green light."

"Shit, you didn't give a red one either."

My dick was hard as hell, wanting to get at her. I knew I couldn't proceed too quickly, though, or she was gonna withdraw altogether. Lifting my hand to her chin, I turned her face to mine. "I won't do anything to this body that you don't want me to do."

My eyes left hers and scanned her body slowly, appreciating the spectacular view that her leggings and thin shirt gave me. "Chinara... you so damn fine and you know that shit."

"I do know, Haji. But... I want to be sure about what I'm doing."

"Understood, but can I kiss you again? That shit was like tasting a fine wine for the first time."

I stared at her lips as my hand rested on her thigh. She nodded and I proceeded with caution, gently grazing her lips with mine before going in for the kill. Kissing wasn't normally my thing because I knew when I met a woman whether I wanted more than sex with her or not. This pretty, black, porcelain doll was in a category all her own. She didn't realize that she possessed the power to have me eating from her palms. I wasn't a soft nigga, but with her... shit, I would be cotton.

My lips connected with hers and I pulled her face closer to mine by the back of her neck. When the soft moan left her lips, I got a little carried away. I pulled her in my lap, and she was cool at first, until I grabbed her ass. She bolted from my lap like all this dick had electrocuted her ass. "This is what can't happen," she said breathlessly.

She left the room and I glanced down at my dick, knowing that I would be jacking off at some point. I wanted to wait until she was comfortable, but I knew that I would probably be fucking somebody else. Jacking off didn't do it for me. I could let that nut off and that muthafucka would still be standing at attention.

I stood from the couch and left the room in search of Chinara. She wasn't in her room, but when I looked across the hallway, I could see her on the balcony. Walking out to her, I knew I owed her an apology. I didn't want it to seem like I was taking advantage of her because she had nowhere else to go. If I had to, I'd ignore her and just do my thang. Standing behind her, I somehow managed to keep my hands to myself and said, "I'm sorry, Chinara. From now on, I'll let you dictate where we go... what we do."

As I was turning to leave, she grabbed my hand, pulling me back to her. She hugged me tightly and laid her head on my chest. I really didn't know what the fuck to do. I was standing there with my arms out in surrender, not wanting to touch her. She whispered, "I'm sorry. I just... this situation is a lot for me right now. I'm trying not to feel used... or like I'm being the user."

Bringing my hands to her shoulders, I gently pushed her away from me. "You would have still been here if I didn't have that situation. So, don't feel used."

She nodded. Whether she was using me or not, I didn't know, but I didn't care. She could keep on using me until she used me up. "Thank you, Haji. You're like my guardian angel."

"Quit saying thank you, man. I don't wanna just be your guardian angel, baby. I wanna be your everything. Since the first day I saw you. I didn't even approach you that first time... just watched this beautiful, black skin walk across the parking lot. When I saw you again, I knew I couldn't let the opportunity to talk to you pass me by. All that was before my dad died. So, relax in this. Pretend that I never asked you to marry me... I mean until we actually go do it."

She giggled and rubbed her hands down my chest. I closed my eyes and shook my head slowly. This shit was gonna be harder than I anticipated. "How long before we do it?"

"Do what?"

My mind was on filling her with this African rod of satisfaction. "Get married."

"Oh, umm... maybe a month from now so it won't look as suspect. My family doesn't know much about my personal life, so they have no idea if I have a girlfriend or not. The last time I was there, I vowed I wouldn't go back."

Chinara had learned a little about my family when we went to lunch at Longhorn Steakhouse. When she'd talked about her parents and sister and how she moved to the country to go to school and had lived with her aunt, I felt like I should tell her a little about my family. All she knew really was that my dad had just died and that my mother and brothers still lived in Freetown. She obviously knew that we were wealthy by my proposal, but I hadn't told her anything about my relationship with any of them, besides my dad. I could see her eyes widen slightly at my admission. "Why?" she asked.

"I feel misunderstood a lot. Because I chose to live my life differently, it was like I was outed by my family, despite my accomplishments. Nothing I did was ever good enough for my father and it was like everyone followed his ideologies. Since I didn't agree with him all the time, my family looked at me as the rebel and somewhat detached from me. My mama talks to me occasionally, but that's about it."

She stepped closer to me and said, "So, you don't really have anyone you can really talk to about things either, huh? I haven't talked to my family in almost three months, but it isn't because we aren't close. My family is poor and they're rooting so hard for me. I didn't want to stress them out by telling them what I'm going through. My mama isn't in the greatest health. I miss them so much."

"Call them. You're good now."

I lifted her hand and kissed it, then walked away before I could give in to my urge to suck her bottom lip. I needed a fucking ice bath.

hinara

As I browned the stew meat, I jammed to Haji's music playing through the speaker system in his house. He'd stepped out for a moment and I took the time to find my way around his kitchen. This moment in my life was surreal. This handsome, rich man was feeling me... wanted me to marry him to get his inheritance, but eluded that if things were good between us, we could stay married. This was so uncomfortable but the most comfortable part about it was that I was so attracted to him.

When he pulled me onto his lap, I could have stripped right then. Feeling a man's erection was like foreign territory. I hadn't been that close to a man in five years. But in all my sexual career of twelve years, I'd never felt a dick so big, powerful-feeling, and desperate for satisfaction. The temptation was so real. Although I was living here, I didn't know Haji. Our situation was unique, but at the same time, I wanted to take things slowly until I got to know him as a person.

His kiss was pure bliss and I wanted to give in to him so badly. When I felt his strong grasp on my ass, I nearly said to hell with it. While it caught me off-guard, it felt good to my soul. Everything about him had me at hello, but I was fighting so hard against him. I was in a position I never wanted to be in again. Needing someone else always made me feel weak, but when their help had stipulations, it made me nervous. Haji said that he was feeling me before he knew about this and I wanted to believe that.

It was hard for me, though, because of my past experiences. All the men I'd had sex with only wanted that one thing. While there had only been three, I'd struck out on love. I was determined to not let another man use me, but in Haji's case... it was like my body was betraying me. It wanted him to use every inch of me for his satisfaction. As I sautéed the vegetables, I couldn't help but let out a soft moan as Rotimi played through the sound system. My body began grooving to the sounds of "Next to Your Love."

I believed he'd put this playlist on intentionally. The song before this was talking about if I was your man. He was seducing me with music. It was working. My panties were so wet, I would surely need a shower once the food was simmering. I'd already cooked the rice in his rice cooker. I turned to look at the huge island in the middle of the kitchen and admired everything about it... imagining myself spread eagle on the white, granite countertop. Quickly turning my head back to the stove, I knew I had to hurry and get this food going. The gushiness between my legs was becoming a bit much.

Right after getting the roux done and adding the meat and vegetables, along with water, I was preparing to head upstairs for a shower. However, Haji walking through the door halted me. I smiled at him and he offered the same. "It smells good in here."

"Thank you."

As I turned to head upstairs, he said, "Chinara, hold on. I have something for you."

I turned back to him in time to see him pulling out a small box.

My eyebrows lifted and he said, "I bought you a ring. Although this is put on... I don't know."

I walked over to him and stood there in front of him with my head down as I watched my mama do over the years with my daddy. I knew what he was trying to say. It felt somewhat real. Sensitivity to him was flowing through me and I knew I needed to get away from him. "Lift your head, Chinara. Look at me. This ain't that old traditional shit."

He smiled, then grabbed my hand and slid the beautiful diamond ring on my finger. It was so gorgeous. When I looked up at him, I said, "Wow. This is beautiful. How did you know my ring size?"

He took one of my rings out of his pocket and handed it to me. "Snatched it up when I was helping you put your things away before I even popped the question," he said, using air quotes, then chuckled.

I smiled then looked back at the ring. Although I knew this wasn't real on the inside, it was definitely real on the outside. "I think we should update our social media pages and post a few pictures of us."

"Okay. What about your women?"

He frowned. "Women?"

"You don't have anybody you kicking it with? You said you weren't celibate."

"Nobody important enough for me to care. It's just sex. You know more about me than any woman I've ever dealt with since I've been here."

"Really?"

"Yeah. Na come on, so we can take this picture."

I giggled, then straightened my hair as he put his arm around my waist, pulling me to him. I smiled big and held my hand up as he took the picture. "You're a great actor," he said as he leaned against the island, staring at me.

"So are you."

I walked away, feeling his eyes bore into my back as I headed up the stairs. As I ascended, I looked over at him to find his eyes on me. I wouldn't last long. My body was ready to offer him the gift without a box or gift bag to put it in. The throbbing in my panties was driving me crazy and it was only going to get worse. Maybe I should just give in. It wasn't like he was a complete stranger. I did know a little bit about him.

Walking into my room, I could hear him coming up the stairs. I could feel the heat around my neck, threatening to choke the shit out of me. Grabbing the scrunchie from the dresser, I pulled my thick hair up as he appeared in the doorway. He didn't say a word and neither did I. When I lowered my hands from my hair, I walked closer to him, then leaned my body against his. His erection was teasing me, but we couldn't do this now. *Could we? No. No. No.* "I just wanted to tell you that I would watch the food, so take your time," he said in a low voice.

He leaned over and softly kissed my neck, pulling me even closer to him, molding my body against his. Slowly, I slid my arms around his waist, then looked up at him. Our attraction was strong, and it seemed like we couldn't quench our desires. Sliding my hands up his body to his face, I pulled him to me and kissed his lips tenderly. When I pulled away, the fire in his eyes all but scorched me.

Slowly backing up, he eased forward, like a puppy begging to be fed. Glancing down at his bulge, I was torn. We weren't a real couple, but it felt like we were. Did I want him to get satisfied elsewhere? I didn't, but why was I putting that on me? As I looked away uncomfortably, Haji said, "I better go back downstairs."

He turned quickly before I could respond. Sliding my hand between my legs, I gripped my sex and whispered, "Oh fuck."

I needed to release, and I knew my body wouldn't calm down until I did. My shit was raging, begging for him to douse my fire. Closing the door, I stripped and immediately slid my finger inside of me. I moaned as I used my other hand to grip one of my nipples. Grinding against my finger, I knew I needed more. Sliding another finger in, I lifted my leg and rested my foot on the bed. My hips instinctively rolled against my digits as my juices rolled from my palm and down to my elbow.

I hadn't been this turned on in years. *What in the fuck was he doing to me?* I wanted to scream out to him to come put me out of my misery, but instead, it came out as a whisper, "Hajiii... yes."

My eyes closed as I finger fucked myself, trying to achieve an orgasm that would cool me off. That would have to suffice for now. The more my fingers penetrated my folds, the faster my hips rolled. I used my thumb to rub circles around my clit and the sensations I felt had me whimpering in satisfaction. "Oh my God," I whispered. "Yes..."

Images of Haji's face between my legs were enough to take me over the edge. My sounds of passion got louder, no matter how I tried to contain them. I practically fell to the floor trying to control the jerks of my body as my orgasm covered my hand. I heard a loud pounding, then a growl from Haji. "Fuck!"

Slowly pulling my fingers from my extremely wet tavern, I wondered if he was jacking off. Going to the bathroom, I turned on the shower, then washed my hand and arm. Going back inside the bedroom, there was a knock at the door. I went to it and answered through the door. "Yes?"

He was quiet for a moment, then he said, "Your whimpers of satisfaction are so sexy. Chinara... damn. Let me have you."

His breathing was heavy and so was mine as I rested my forehead against the door. "Let me take your body places that you can't. I promise I'm gon' be ten times better than your fingers were. Let me in, Pretty Black."

His voice was low and steady, and it caressed every part of me. Resting my fingers on the doorknob, I thought hard about what we were about to do. My pussy was ready for sure, but my heart wasn't. My heart needed more assurance that this wouldn't be over once he got what he wanted... not me, but his inheritance. Just him calling me pretty black made me wanna see what that bow in is legs was all about.

I could hear him breathing as he waited for my decision. Just as I was about to open the door, he said, "It's okay. I know you aren't ready. Whenever you are, you free to hop on this dick anytime, anyplace. I promise to take you to ecstasy every time, Pretty Black Doll."

I could hear him walk away and I wanted to melt to the floor. *Why didn't I say anything?* I was so fucking horny; I could pass out from desire. But something inside of me wouldn't allow me to give in to him. Even though thoughts of him had led to the best self-pleasuring session I'd ever had. If thoughts of him could do that, then I knew the real thing would probably kill me. My body was sacred to me, though. I needed some sort of commitment before surrendering to him. If he said that I was the only woman for him, then I'd lay before him, allowing him to do with me as he pleased. Attraction... desire... lust... none of that was enough for me.

Finally making my way to the shower, I couldn't deal with how hot it was anymore. My shit was still contracting from the aftershocks. The shower would be for nothing if I was in a full sweat when I got out. Haji could have it all. Getting to know his heart was more overwhelming than I had imagined. He was intelligent and could flip the script in a minute. I learned that just from conversation. He could sound like a thug from the American streets or a highly cultured, intellectual man from London.

His accent was somewhat of a mix. Since Sierra Leone was once inhabited by the British, a lot of natives had that accent mixed with their African accent. Haji was just everything a woman could want. The only issue for me was the casual sex. Hopefully, he was wrapping up. As I washed, I thought about what my plan would be. I still would continue to look for a job. Although he said I didn't have to work, I needed to be able to provide for myself. When the seven to eight months were over, what if we couldn't stand each other?

Getting out, I quickly dressed in an oversized shirt and leggings, then made my way downstairs to check on the food. Haji was stirring the pot, wearing basketball shorts and a wife beater. *Dear God.* His biceps were shining like he'd rubbed oil on them. He was so damn sexy. Turning to me, he stared at me, slowly licking his lips. "I think it's ready."

Using the spoon, he scooped up some for me to taste. He blew it to cool it off but incited a whole new fire within me. I sipped it from the spoon and closed my eyes as I savored the taste. "Mmm. It is. Let me prepare you a plate."

"Chinara, I can fix my own food. Let me fix yours, though."

I stared at him as he went got a couple of bowls from his cabinet. Once he spooned rice in both bowls, he went to the stove to fill our bowls with beef stew. I'd put potatoes and carrots in it as well. The seasoning was perfect. I never got it right on the first attempt, but I guess there was a first time for everything. I was waiting for him to bring up what happened before our showers, but he didn't say a word. Bringing our bowls to the table, he smiled at me and said, "So, I'm glad you can cook. Maybe I won't have to eat fast food so often. Sometimes when I get off work, I don't feel like cooking."

"I love to cook."

Pulling his wallet from his pocket, he took a card out of it and slid it to me. "This is for whatever you might need. I go back to work Monday. So, if there's something you need, you can use this. I also need a list of your bills so I can pay them."

I fidgeted in my seat some, but I didn't pick up the card. This shit made me so uncomfortable. "I don't wanna make a habit of being forceful with you, Chinara. Take the card. I expect to have that list tonight. I know for sure you have a car note, insurance, and a phone bill. Hit me with all of it."

I swallowed hard as I looked at the credit card. He stretched out his hand and I put mine in his. As he blessed the food, I couldn't help but think about how blessed I was. Just when I thought God had forgotten about me, he sent Haji to my rescue. Taking a deep breath, I looked at him and said, "Okay. Besides the bills you mentioned, I have a storage bill for my aunt's furniture."

"That's it? I want even the minor shit like XM Satellite or Apple Music or whatever."

"Okay, Haji."

I smiled at him as he stood to get our drinks. Instead of being uptight, I supposed I should just thank God for the elevation and keep my previous mantra when I didn't have the help. Worry about tomorrow when it got here.

aji

CHINARA HAD PUT her foot in that damn stew. It was so good. I already knew that I would boil her some seafood tomorrow. Remembering how her stomach growled in the store that day when she looked at it on the conveyor belt still plagued me. She was starving that day. I never looked at being able to buy groceries as a privilege until that day.

Sliding that ring on her finger felt right as hell. I knew sliding in between her walls would feel right as well, but I would do that shit on her timing. Her moans took me down earlier. I had to go jack off just to get the edge off. I'd hit the wall and had to verbalize my satisfaction. I came so hard in that toilet, my knees had buckled. Thoughts of her... making love to her... fucking her, had me like a damn hound dog on her scent.

After we finished eating and cleaning up, she sat at the table and made a list of her bills on her phone, then sent it to me, along with how to pay them. What she had was less than eight hundred a month. Since neither of us had a thing to do tomorrow, I brought her to the couch and let her pick a movie for us to watch. After picking *Love Jones*, she snuggled into me. Putting my arm around her, I found myself praying for strength because being this close to her as badly as I was fiending for a taste was torture.

I found myself playing in her hair just so I didn't see the romantic moments playing out on the screen, but I found that wasn't any better. When Nia Long's character and Larenz Tate began making love, she looked up at me, then ran her fingers through my beard. I laid my head back and closed my eyes, biting my bottom lip. I needed to get in some slick shit, for real. She slid her hand over my cheek and pulled my face down. "You can change the movie. I wasn't thinking."

"It's cool. We can watch it. You just can't be moaning all loud and shit when you masturbate tonight. I had to jack off. And to be clear... I'm not complaining about anything, but I never beg. You had a nigga willing to give a lung to slide in that pussy, Pretty Black."

The light from the TV allowed me to see the goosebumps on her arms, but I also heard her breathing go shallow. I leaned over and kissed her neck, then nibbled at her ear, torturing my damn self. We were going to have to stay away from moments like this. She turned to me and laid those pretty lips on mine, slipping her tongue inside my mouth, giving me life with its every stroke against mine. I squeezed her thigh, then quickly pulled away from her. "See, I know you craving that intimacy shit right now, but I can't go that far with my intimacy. My dick hard as shit right now."

"Haji... have you been tested?"

"What?"

"For STD's. Have you had blood work done?"

"Naw. I wrap up all the time, but if that's something you need, I can make it happen."

"Yeah, I do."

"A'ight."

I focused back on the movie or at least I tried to. Most times, I found my eyes closed, wanting to stroke my dick. I was so tempted to make a call, but I said I would never dip back to Kyley's ass. If I couldn't go a good week without sex, then I had a problem. I'd gone weeks before, but I didn't have temptation living with me, taunting me at every turn. But she had best believe, I was getting that blood test. "Pretty Black, I want to be with you and only you, but this gon' be hard. I dream and fantasize about you and I have been since I saw you. You always on my mind and it's making me crazy."

She sat up on the couch and looked at me. "Is that your way of letting me know that you will be fucking other women? I mean... I already assumed that. We aren't a couple. But you don't have to try to pressure me into something I told you I wasn't ready for."

I frowned. "Whoa... what?"

Sitting up on the sofa, I watched her fold her arms. I could sense her slight attitude from here. "Ain't nobody pressuring you into shit. I'm just explaining how bad I want you. I want you to be mine, but I know you ain't going for that right now 'cause you don't know me well enough yet. I'm not complaining. Man... fuck it."

I stood from the sofa and sat the remote on the couch, then headed upstairs. Explaining myself wasn't something I did. She must didn't hear a word I said all day. I didn't have to pressure her. Good pussy came a dime a dozen, but I was trying to wait for her. It had only been a day for her. I got that. It was harder for me because I had been fantasizing about her ass for two months. She was tripping already.

When I got to my room, I pulled some jeans from the hanger and sent Kyley a message. *You home?*

After putting them on and slipping on a white tee, she messaged me back. *Yeah, daddy. You coming through?*

On my way, lil mama.

I brushed my waves, sprayed a little cologne, then headed back downstairs. Chinara was turning off the TV. When she turned to me, her eyebrows lifted, then she frowned. "I'll be back."

I didn't give her anything more. She expected me to fuck around, so be it. I chose her because I felt something special when I looked at her. Any woman would have been willing to do what I asked of her. I asked her for a reason, though. I thought she was the woman that I could build something with. But in my book, there was a such thing as being too strong sometimes. She was stubborn and she was acting like me going fuck somebody else didn't bother her. Since she wanted to act that way, I'd take it at face value and do that shit.

When I backed out the driveway, I was pissed. *Why I let her get to me like that?* Like she said, we weren't a couple. I thought she wanted to build up to that like I did. Apparently, I was wrong. Taking the ten-minute drive to Kyley's apartment, I sat in the parking lot for a moment. I grabbed my phone, for some reason, expecting a message from her to make me go back home. Wrong again. I got out the car and went to let Kyley get me off. Hopefully, she wasn't on that same bullshit she was on the other day. When I knocked on the door, she opened it wearing a see-through catsuit. "Hey, daddy. Come in, so I can service that big-ass dick."

Shit. Happy Kwanza, Haji.

I HAD BEEN AVOIDING Chinara all day. When I got home last night, she was in her room and I could hear the music playing. I went straight to my room and took a shower and didn't bother to come back out. Kyley had fucked me right. I nutted three times... one for each hole. She put in work last night and I was completely satisfied until I got home. Chinara was the woman I wanted but couldn't really have. I knew I was probably playing a dangerous game by fooling around with Kyley again, but I was angry and made an irrational decision to give me relief at the moment.

When I woke up this morning, I could hear her moving around and turning the shower on, so I quickly got dressed and went to the corner store to get bacon, egg, and cheese croissants and a couple of pastries, then came back and ate in my room. Around noon, I finally decided to come out and quit hiding out in my own house. Jarius said he would be over when he left the shop, and my boy Kline was coming over in an hour.

I had water boiling outside on a propane burner and had put vegetables in it along with seasoning, getting ready to boil shrimp and snow crabs. I'd probably throw in some sausage, potatoes, corn on the cob, pork bones, and ham hocks. Kline had said he was gonna bring rabbit and deer meat to put in there. I was all for it. He was from one of the rural areas around Beaumont called Hillebrandt. They were always hunting, especially rabbit hunting. When he got here, I'd put that stuff at the bottom to tenderize it.

By the time Jarius and his boy from the shop, Jamel, got here, the food would all be cooked. When I walked back into the house, Chinara was standing in the kitchen. It looked like she had been watching me through the window. I nodded at her and said, "What's up?"

"Hey."

When she pushed her hair away from her face, her ring caught my attention. "You know you don't have to wear it around the house, just when we're out."

She nodded, then said, "I want to wear it."

I shrugged and was walking to the utility room to get a couple of coolers when she said, "I'm sorry about last night."

Stopping my forward progress, I turned to her. She averted her gaze to the floor, like she was embarrassed. "Sorry for what?"

"I snapped on you for no reason. I guess I'm just scared of what's happening between us. I'm feeling you, Haji. I'm sure you know that. But I'm afraid that I won't be able to please you."

Tilting my head to the side, I frowned. "Why do you think that?"

"Because... umm... you are extremely sexual. I haven't had sex in five years. When I have sex again, I want it to be with someone I want forever with."

"Says the woman wearing an engagement ring. I could have asked anybody to marry me. For what I'm offering, I know a few who would have jumped on the opportunity. I asked you, because I see something in you... feel something about you that makes me want more. It makes me wanna know more. I don't know what that something is yet, but I plan to find out. I'm gon' do better about rushing into sex. I said I would let you make the first move in that direction, so I'm gonna honor that."

"But... how will this work? If I'm not giving it to you, you're gonna get it elsewhere."

"Tell me what you want me to do, Chinara."

I walked closer to her, wanting her to tell me that she wanted my devotion and loyalty. I needed her to express how she felt for me and what she expected from me. Turning her head to look out the window for a moment, she turned back to me and said, "I can't... I can't tell you what I want if I'm not willing to offer you what you want."

When I got close enough to her, I lifted her chin to where she could look into my eyes. "Tell. Me. What. You. Want. Me. To. Do."

"I... I want you to stop fucking other women. Haji, but that's not fair to you. I want more with you. Having you as mine is a feeling that I want to treasure forever."

I couldn't help but kiss her after that. She wanted the same things I did, and it took me going fuck somebody else for her to admit it. *Women.* Sliding my hands to her face, I gently stroked her cheeks with my thumbs, then kissed that sexy ring in her nose. "You got that, Pretty Black Doll."

I knew her feelings were out of excitement because there was still so much more we needed to know about one another. With the shit I had already shown her, it made her want to know more and I could get with that. The situation was making her move a lot quicker as well. Living with me, seeing my comings and goings could affect her one of two ways. Either she could fall in love with me or she could eventually hate me.

I was never a nigga to hide shit, so leaving when I did last night, she knew I was going get my dick wet, no question. Being

CHAPTER 9 | 67

discreet had never been my thing because I never really had anyone's feelings to worry about. I'd never had a girlfriend. My forehead was against hers and I couldn't seem to separate from her until I heard, "Nigga, you gon' boil all the water out the pot or what?"

Stepping away from Chinara, I saw Kline standing there with his eyebrows lifted and a goofy-ass smile on his face. He had two bags in his hands, which I was sure was the rabbit and deer meat. "Kline, this is my woman, Chinara."

"Woman? What the hell?" He walked to the sink and sat the bags in it, then washed his hands. "My bad, Chinara. I'm just in shock."

When he reached out to shake her hand, she extended the hand with the ring on it. I knew she did that on purpose. No one really shook hands with their left hand unless the right one was unavailable for some reason. His eyes widened as he yelled, "Y'all engaged??"

"Yeah. Quit tripping," I said.

He and I didn't talk every day, but he usually knew what was going on with me. The only person that knew about the arrangement and the situation I was in was Jarius. I pulled Chinara back to me and kissed her lips. She looked up at me and said, "You need me to wash the meat?"

"Yeah, please?"

Kline was still standing there in shock as I continued to the utility room to get the coolers. When I walked back out, he was standing outside near the pot. As soon as I got out there, he went in. "When the fuck you had time to find a woman and propose to her since the last time we talked?"

"Man, shut yo' country ass up."

After sitting the coolers down, I went back inside to get the meat from Chinara. She'd put it in a pan. I smiled at her and she returned the smile and asked, "Are you gonna tell him the truth?"

"Nope. The only person that knows is Jarius."

"Is that the one from the barbershop?"

"Yeah. He's my barber."

"So... umm, can I go outside with you guys? Or should I stay inside?"

I frowned at her, then pulled her to me by her waist. "You are welcome to be anywhere that I am. We have a lot to talk about and I want you to feel comfortable expressing yourself to me. Treat this like you would treat any other relationship. Despite that we'll be married next month and we live together, the progress of our feelings will be the same. You feel me?"

She slid her hands up to my face and said, "I feel you."

She kissed my lips, then grabbed my phone and cued up the music through the sound system. When "Shawty" by Plies started playing, she started swaying to the music. "I haven't heard this in a *long* time!"

I chuckled at her, then grabbed the meat to put in the pot before I pushed *my* meat against her ass. Following me outside, she watched me use the long spoon to put the meat in the water. Once I put it all in, I dropped some shrimp and crab in on top of it, along with potatoes, corn, and sausage. Kline was still staring at me like I was a damn stranger and it caused me to laugh. "Kline, close your mouth before some flies drop some eggs in there."

hinara

As I SAT on Haji's lap, I realized that I had completely relaxed in us. He and his boys were talking and laughing as they puffed on cigars and I was eating for the second time. Everything was so delicious. I'd never eaten rabbit or deer meat, but I knew for sure it wouldn't be my last time eating it. I was thankful that they'd cooked so much, so I could have some tomorrow. Jarius and I had talked quite a bit. He felt like he knew me since he and Haji talked so often.

Haji wrapped his arms around me and kissed my back and I couldn't help but smile. I couldn't believe he was gonna make the effort to give me what I asked for. When he left last night, I threw up. Thinking about him fucking somebody else made me sick to my stomach. That was weird as hell to me. I supposed subconsciously, because I was living with him, I felt like he was mine. I took what he'd said the wrong way. I should have taken it as a compliment that he wanted me so badly but was willing to wait.

He had no intent to leave the house last night until I over analyzed what he'd said and threw my attitude out there. I could tell it pissed him off immediately. Humbling myself today had been hard, but it got me where I wanted to be... sitting on his lap, enjoying good food and fun conversation with his friends. As Kirko Bangz came on, I wiggled my ass again. Feeling his slight erection, I stopped. Turning to him, I mouthed, *sorry*.

Giving me a one-cheeked smile, I could see the wheels turning in his head. Taking a puff from his cigar, he sat up and slid his hand to my thigh, continuing to talk to his friends. When I was done eating, I told his friends bye and made my way inside. I began washing pans and loading the dishwasher. I'd mop once everyone left. The food was all still sitting out, so I transferred it all to containers and put it in the fridge.

When I was done, I headed upstairs to take a shower. I'd had an amazing time with Haji and his friends today, but I knew they wanted to talk and kick it without me being out there. I wasn't out there the entire time, but after our short talk earlier, I wanted to be as close to Haji as possible. I still hadn't posted our pictures to our social media. I wanted to talk to my family first. Being that it had gotten late, I knew my parents were asleep.

After taking my shower and washing my hair, I stood in the mirror detangling it, applying product, and putting it in bantu knots. The knock on the door caused me to put on a housecoat and tie at it at my waist. "Come in."

When Haji walked in, he smiled at me. "Damn, you smell good."

I smiled at him, then tiptoed to kiss his lips. "I like how you relaxed in this, Pretty Black. It feels good, huh?" he asked as he stood behind me, wrapping his arms around me.

"It really does."

Letting my guard down was scary, but now that I had, it felt amazing. Releasing me, he said, I'm gonna go take a shower, then we can talk. A'ight?"

"Okay."

He kissed my head and left the bathroom as I continued doing my hair. I was almost done, then I would go mop the kitchen. Because of the amazing day we had, I knew our talk would go well. I just didn't know what we needed to talk about that we hadn't already worked out throughout the day. I knew that he'd put pictures on his social media pages of us and people were asking all sorts of questions and congratulating him on our engagement. He wouldn't be able to pull no shit like he did last night anymore, regardless of how I was behaving... not if he wanted people to take our engagement seriously.

Once I finished my hair, I went downstairs and found the mop bucket, just as Haji was joining me. He smiled, then started the water running so it could get hot. Getting the Clorox from the washroom, I poured a little in the bucket as he frowned slightly. "Clorox is going to get this floor cleaner than any other product you can use. Watch."

He lifted his hands in surrender with a slight smile. Detaching the faucet, he ran the hot water in the bucket. After dipping the mop a couple of times and ringing it out, I began and he went to the couch in the family room. He started the music again. Nothing harsh but the smooth sounds of Tank. I gathered that he liked music a lot. There was rarely a quiet moment when he was here. I loved music too, so I was cool with it. After finishing the floor, I yelled, "Haji! Come see!"

When he walked to the kitchen, his eyebrows lifted. "Damn. You were right. It looks good. Thank you, Pretty Black."

He went to the mop bucket and picked it up, carrying it outside to the patio. Once he poured the water over the spot where he had the pot, he rinsed the bucket with the hose, then came back inside the house. Meeting me in the washroom, he set the bucket down as I hung the mop, then grabbed my hand. When we got to the couch, he pulled me in his lap. "Today was so chill."

"It was. I enjoyed relaxing with you, Haji."

"I'm glad you did. I just want things to flow naturally with us."

Laying my head against his shoulder, he wrapped his other arm around me. "My brother commented on my picture. I know I'm gonna have to call sooner or later. When I do, if you could just walk in the background a couple of times, that'll be cool."

I giggled. "Okay."

"So... tell me about your love life. Why are you so guarded?"

I shifted in his lap, then traced his bottom lip with my finger. "I've always been the one whose love was taken advantage of, starting from my first boyfriend in high school to the one I broke up with five years ago. There have only been three, but every last one of them played me for a fool. Although I was a teenager with the first one, my feelings for him were real. I was naturally a loving person. They took that from me. I changed into someone I wasn't. Becoming skeptical of every damn thing is so exhausting at times, especially with you."

"Well, I know I gave you a reason to be skeptical and I'm sorry."

"Can I ask you a question?"

"Yeah. What's up?" he asked as he pulled me closer.

"Did you actually go fuck somebody last night? Or did you just leave to make me think you were?"

He slid his hand down his face as he exhaled. No words needed to be spoken at that point. I knew that he had. Before he could answer, I put my fingers over his lips. He kissed them, then grabbed them from his lips. "You don't have to explain. I got it."

"As long as we're on this path we're on, it'll be the last time. I promise."

Despite my past with men, I believed him. He could have lied to me just now, but he didn't. I respected him even more for that. "So, tell me about your brothers."

"Kevin is a thorn in my flesh. He's two years older than me and constantly looks for something he can expose about me. He's blocked from all my social media accounts. When I saw him while I was out there, that was my first time talking to him in over two years. My oldest brother, Umaru, is cool. He's just a follower. I mean of Ense. Whatever my father told him to do was the right thing in his book. Anyone that went against that was wrong. We get along, though. He still respects me for the most part."

I could tell that it pained him to talk about his family and I hated that for him. I'd always had my family's love and support. They knew that coming to America was the best thing for me. Rubbing my hand over his face, I said, "Well, I still can't wait to meet them and your mother."

He'd already told me about his parents, mainly his father. I knew from that conversation that he held a lot of anger inside because of the things his father did and said to him. Haji held resentment in his heart also because of the things his father *didn't* say to him. I knew he and his mother were close at some point, but since his dad had died, things had been awkward. He kissed my cheek and said, "I'm not gonna be like your past relationships. Although I've never been in a real relationship, I'm determined to make this between us work. I'm ready to fall in love and have a family, I just hadn't met the right person to do that with until I met you."

My heart was pierced and the blood from it was healing me from the inside out. Sitting up in his arms, I straddled him. He averted his gaze and I knew he wanted me to move, but I refused. I put my hands on both sides of his face, forcing him to look at me. After kissing his lips, I said, "Haji?"

He rested his hands on my back, then slid them to my hips as he stared at my chest. "Mmm-hmm."

"Touch me..."

He licked his lips and brought his hands to my neck, gently squeezing it as I closed my eyes. A soft moan left my lips, then he pulled me closer to him. His hands slid around to my back and he gripped my ass like he did yesterday. A soft groan left his lips as I wrapped my arms around his neck. I just wanted to be free to decide what I wanted without living in fear of what could happen. Just like I was in everyday life, I wanted to be that way in relationships as well. Feeling his touch moved me in ways unfathomable and I wanted to explore more. "Haji," I whispered.

"Pretty Black, you know what this can lead to. I don't think you're ready yet."

He slid his hands in my leggings and grabbed my bare ass and the moan that left me shocked even me with how passionate it sounded. When he stood with me in his arms, I opened my eyes and wrapped my legs around him, staring into his eyes like I'd seen God. Going up the stairs, he passed my room and went straight to his, then laid me on the bed. I was so ready to give him all of me. It even felt like my tights were wet.

Haji hovered over me with his clothes still on and kissed me like I was a priceless jewel deep from the mines of Sierra Leone. When his lips traveled to my neck, I couldn't help but hold his head there, letting him saturate me in what he was feeling for me... tenderness, care, and affection. Lifting his head, he stared at me and said, "I want to please you, Chinara, but I don't want you changing your mind about what you said. I'm prepared to wait. I don't plan to leave you like this, though."

"Haji... pleeeaase take me," I moaned as I arched my back.

He slid his fingers down my chest to the waistband of my pants, then lifted my hips and pulled them down, taking my underwear with them. Kissing my legs as he pulled my garments over my feet, he moaned. Feeling his lips ascend my calf, I opened my eyes to look at him. When he got in view of my pussy, he spread my legs open wider and stared at it. I was trembling, wanting him to kill the foreplay and teasing. "Damn, she's beautiful," he whispered.

When he got close to where I needed him most, I could feel him breathing on it, taking in her scent, when he suddenly tongue kissed her. I picked my hips up to his mouth, trying to drown him in my juices as he gently sucked the inner lips of my pussy. "Hajiii... oh my God."

His tongue licked my opening like it was leaking maple syrup, then shortly after he slid his fingers inside as his mouth went to my clit. He moaned out his indulgence as he stroked me, caressing my G-spot. I felt like I was about to levitate because my climax was near. Not having a man to make me feel this pleasure in five years, then to be met with a fucking professional at the sport, had me about to climb the walls. I held his head as I lifted from the bed to watch him.

That only made what I was feeling more intense. Taking his fingers from me, he sucked them, then said, "You taste better than I fucking imagined, Pretty Black. I could suck on your fruit all damn day."

I was about to erupt. My body was screaming for relief and Haji was on the verge of getting me there. But now he was only staring at it, begging it to freely give him what he wanted instead of him having to take it. "Chinara, cum for me, baby. Give daddy that B-12," he said softly against my pussy, producing a chill that ran through my body.

He was purposely prolonging my orgasm, making me feel like I was on the verge of insanity. Slowly, he slid his fingers back inside of me, then laid his lips on my clit and hummed. "Oooooh!" I screamed.

Just like that, I was right back on the verge of giving it all to him. He began sucking my clit as he massaged my G-spot and my orgasm broke through like water at a compromised damn. My screams only fueled Haji's assault and he licked and sucked me faster, flattening his tongue whenever he could. Once the feeling subsided, he kissed my inner thighs and said, "I can't wait to make love to this tight pussy."

He licked his lips, then stood from the bed, going to the bathroom. I was somewhat confused because I was waiting to feel him inside of me. When he came back with a towel, I wanted to cry. He must have seen the disappointment on my face because a smirk appeared on his lips. "What's wrong, Chinara?"

"I want more."

"Naw. I gotta get the blood test Monday, remember? Plus, you ain't ready."

"I'm sooo ready. You gon' make me beg?"

"It won't change things."

Glancing down at his crotch, I could see how hard he was. "Let me help that rocket take off. It's full of fuel and just need to be ignited. Let me, Haji."

He gently cleaned me up with an amused look on his face. "Chinara, when I give you all this dick, you gon' be telling me shit you ain't ready to tell me, whether it's in your mouth or in this fat pussy. I realized what you needed when you were talking. You need me to take things slow. So tomorrow, we're going on a date."

He'd never looked in my eyes while he was talking. His eyes stayed on the object of his affection. I knew he wanted me, but because of me being scared, he was gonna make me wait. But to have to wait after the tongue lashing he'd just given me was torture. I wanted more. "Haji, I'm ready. I need to feel you... please."

He stood to his feet and yanked me from the bed. My eyes widened as my pussy throbbed, hoping that he would fill it. He walked to the nearest wall and almost threw me against it. My legs tightened around him as he watched our pelvises meet. Rolling my hips against him, I could see my juices leaking on his pants. "You don't want to feel all this wrapped around you, Haji?"

"You know I do. But I don't want you to regret it. I want you to be sure you're ready... clear-headed. Right now, you soaring from the head you just got... above the damn clouds."

Letting me slide to the floor, he left the room quick as hell. Doing my best to go after him on wobbly legs, I saw him enter the hallway bathroom and close the door. Walking down the hallway, I heard him grunting, just as he heard me last time. I knocked on the door, then rested my head against it. Like him, I'd never begged a man for his dick, but shit, I needed it. I didn't have a dildo to somewhat quench my thirst. "Haji..."

He opened the door and it looked like his dick was hanging to his fucking knees. I knew that those legs were bowed out like that for a reason. My mouth immediately watered. "This that shit you want, Pretty Black. You sure you ready for this? It's gon' have you speaking in languages you didn't even know you knew. Go get a condom out of my nightstand drawer."

I was in a trance, though. He was stroking it and it was dripping excellence that I wanted to lay up under and catch... every drop. The desire that I felt was foreign to me. He walked closer to me as my breathing picked up and asked, "You gon' go get it or what?"

He rubbed his dick against my stomach, and I reached out to grab it. Slapping my hand, he said, "Condom, before I change my mind about fucking up yo' insides."

I nearly ran to the bedroom. That veiny muscle looked like it was strong enough to handle a demolition all by itself... pure wrecking-ball status. I hurriedly grabbed a condom and got back to him in record time. He snatched the condom from me and tore it open. The calm, tender demeanor he had before was long gone and I was scared for my virgin-like pussy. Once he slid it on, he yanked me to him and picked me up. "No turning back, no regrets, no crawfishing. At this point, after I penetrate this pussy, it's mine... whenever I want it, wherever I need it."

I nodded quickly, holding my breath. While I expected him to penetrate me roughly, he slowly lowered me on him. The slow stretching of my insides to accommodate his size was painful but I knew it would be worth it in just a few minutes. I pulled my shirt over my head and Haji immediately pulled my nipple into his mouth as he lowered me more. "Oh shit!" I yelled.

My nails had already begun to dig into his shoulders. Lifting me slightly, he began a slow rhythm that felt so damn good, I was literally speechless. My screams and words were unintelligible, and I'd forgotten English altogether. "Oluwa mi o! Fokii mi!"

Apparently, Haji understood Yoruba and knew that I'd said, *Oh my God! Fuck me!* He lowered me more on his dick and I knew he'd bypassed my cervix. I wrapped my arms around his neck and sank my teeth into his shoulder. "I'm sorry. You okay?"

"Yes," I whispered as the tears fell from my eyes. "Keep going."

I thought at that point I had taken it all. Knowing that he had more that hadn't experienced the warmth and tightness of my walls somewhat deflated me. I tried not to think about not being able to satisfy him, but I couldn't help it. However, when he lifted me again and began working his dick inside of me, the feelings of enjoyment were returning. Walking down the hallway to his room, he said, "I'm sorry, Chinara. I didn't mean to hurt you."

"Shhh."

He laid me on the bed, then climbed atop me. "Do you want to continue?"

When he saw the tears in my eyes, he wiped them and rolled over to the bed. "Haji, I want you to continue. It may be painful this time, but next time will be better. Please, don't stop," I said as I rubbed his chest.

Hovering back over me, he stared into my eyes as he slowly pushed inside of me, biting his bottom lip. His slow pace felt good and this position seemed to be easier for me to handle. As he worked into a nice rhythm, he grabbed my neck and hooked my leg with his other arm. "This better, baby?"

"Yeah. So... much... better," I panted.

When he pushed more into me, it wasn't as painful and I was able to handle it, but my disappointment with myself was floating through my head. How could I place stipulations on who he fucked? I couldn't handle all of him and that fucked with my mental.

aji

"Relax. I can see you're tense, Chinara. I understand that it's been five years and this shit ain't yo' average-sized dick."

I smiled at her and swiped the tears from her eyes. As I pulled out of her, my dick screamed. I didn't nut because I could see she was in pain. I'd tried to give her too much at once. I hated that because her pussy felt so damn good. Getting up from the bed, I went to the bathroom and ran her some bathwater, then threw the condom in the wastebasket. I sat on the edge of the tub and thought about how I should have waited. I shouldn't have let her pressure me into fucking her yet. She wasn't ready to be fucked.

Going back to the room, I helped her from the bed and pulled her in my arms. "Don't cry. I was too rough and anxious to get inside of you. Next time will be better. Okay?"

She nodded and I led her to the bathroom. I'd have to get at her before I got so worked up like I was. That way I could take things slow with her. I felt horrible. "Just soak for a while, baby. You need anything?"

She shook her head, but I was sure she could use a drink. I kissed her forehead, then left her in the bathroom. Going downstairs, I poured her a glass of wine, then set the alarm and made my way back up. She'd gotten in the tub, so I handed the wine to her and sat the bottle on the floor next to her. This shit was my fault. I should have known better. Rubbing my hand down my face, I sat on the edge of the bed. My phone began ringing and when I saw Jarius's number, I grabbed it and left the room. "What's up?" I answered.

"If I didn't know any better, I'd think y'all were in love. That shit looked so natural."

"It was natural, man. She my woman, for real."

"Damn! Yo' slick ass! We gon' have to hook up so we can talk freely. That ring is nice, though."

"Thanks, bruh. We definitely gon' have to hook up, but it may have to wait until next weekend when I come to get my cut."

"You a'ight? You sound kind of... I don't know... upset about something."

"We'll talk next week. But I need to go check on Pretty Black."

"She's beautiful, Haji. I'm glad things may work out for the best after all."

"Thanks, bruh. Talk to you later."

"A'ight."

Making my way back to my bedroom, I could hear that Chinara was still in the tub. I thought I was gonna be able to jack off, but my dick was completely flaccid now. Just knowing I'd hurt her had taken my drive. He wasn't even tryna wake up now. I should have known better than starting in the position I started in with her. *Damn.* It was too late for regrets, though. I just needed to make sure that she knew it wasn't her fault and that we would get where we needed to be next time... whenever she was ready to try again.

She was so fucking wet, though. Even though she was hurting, her pussy was still lubing that condom up. I could feel her juices leaking to my balls. Her facial expressions and her tears are what caused me to stop. Had I not seen that I would have nutted all in that shit.

After another thirty minutes, I could hear her letting the water out of the tub. I stood to go help her get situated. Knocking on the door, she opened it for me, already in her nightshirt. The glass was empty and upon further inspection, the bottle was practically empty, too. She smiled at me and said, "You wanna try again?"

"Naw. You better get some rest. Let's give it a couple of days and give that sweet pussy time to recuperate."

"You sure?"

"I'm more than sure. You deserve better."

"So do you."

"Let me help you to bed."

"Can I sleep with you?"

"You a lil tipsy, Chinara. You sure you want to?"

"Yep. I just wanna lay close to you and let you hold me in your arms."

"A'ight."

I led her to my bed, then plugged my charger up to my phone. This would be a first for me. Holding a woman all night in my bed had never happened. I refused to allow it. Now my heart was giddy with excitement to feel her next to me. It gave me a sense of need... like she needed me to protect her, take care of her, and comfort her. For now, that satisfaction was enough.

———

"What's this I see on your page? I didn't know you had a girlfriend and now you are engaged to be married?"

"No one ever asked. You all just assume that you know every aspect of my life. I let all of you keep your assumptions."

I'd FaceTimed my brother Umaru and he happened to be at Mama's house, which was perfect. Kevin's ass was there, too. Just as

Mama's face appeared on the screen, Chinara walked by in the background as we had discussed she would do. Mama's eyes widened. "Is that her, pikin? She's more beautiful than any uman you could have found in Salone."

She often mixed Krio dialect within her English. Pikin meant child and uman meant woman. I smiled slightly because she was right. Chinara was the most beautiful woman I'd ever seen, that included in Salone and the U.S. "That's her. Her name is Chinara."

"Can she come to the phone? Is she from Texas?"

"She's from Lagos."

The wide-eyed expression on my mother's face made me smile even more. They thought they knew so much about me. But they didn't know a got damn thing. "Pretty Black Doll," I called out.

Umaru's face brightened at my nickname for her. "Yeah, baby?"

"My family would like to meet you."

She smiled and made her way to me, sitting on the couch beside me. Leaning over, she kissed my cheek, then looked at the camera and smiled big. *All of her belonged to me.* Chinara was so beautiful. She left me in awe every time she smiled. Even in a t-shirt and wind shorts, with her hair piled atop her head, she was the sexiest woman alive. "Wow... Kusheh," my mama said, clearly in awe of Chinara's beauty.

"Kusheh," Chinara said back.

"Mama, she doesn't speak the language fluently. She speaks English, Yoruba, Igbo, and Hausa."

"I apologize, Chinara. You're so beautiful."

"No problem. Thank you so much. I see where Haji gets his good looks from."

My mama blushed as Kevin brought his slick ass into view. I put my arm around Chinara and stared at her like they weren't on the phone. "You sure this ain't fake? You probably struck a deal with her to get your money."

Chinara frowned harder than she did when I first tried to talk to her, calling her Pretty Black Doll. She quickly took the phone from my hand as she stared at him with fire in her eyes. "Nothing is fake about how I feel for this man. How dare you question something you know nothing about?"

She stood from her seat next to me, gave me my phone, and walked off. Chinara was angry for real. It was sort of played up. There was no way we would be engaged already if it weren't for the foolery with my dad's will. When I looked back at the screen, Kevin was gone. Umaru had a frown on his face as did Mama. Seeing Chinara's frown affected them. Her frowns affected me, too. But I knew they were sort of embarrassed by what he said. She'd gone to the kitchen and was warming us some food from the boil yesterday. That deer meat and rabbit were so tender and good. Neither of us could get enough of it.

"Apologize to Chinara, please," Umaru said. "When is the wedding?"

"I don't know exactly. We probably won't have a wedding. Neither of us have a lot of people here that we're that close to. It will just be a one-day decision to go to the courthouse and do it."

I looked up at Chinara and winked at her. She smiled brightly at me, causing me to smile, too. Neither of us had veered away from one another last night. I could remember in my sleep that if I felt her getting away from me, I'd pull her back. Caressing her body in her sleep was everything... listening to her soft moans as I did so had me readier than ready. So, I eventually had to stop. Feeling her against me all night was soothing as hell. She didn't wake up one time during the night. I knew that wine had her feeling lovely.

Chinara sat our plates on the table and I realized I'd been staring at her the entire time. Looking back at my phone, my mama was smiling and Umaru said, "You got it bad, bruh."

I smiled slightly. He was right. Chinara had me tripping. Everything about her was perfect, from her thick, kinky-curly hair, to her suck-able toes.

Her fiery temperament and sensitivity.

Her innocence and dirty mouth.

Those perfect titties that adorned damn near black nipples only turned me on. Her ass was the perfect peach, giving me something to grab and fiend over. "Bad ain't the word to describe it."

He and Mama laughed, bringing my attention back to them. "Well, I have to go. Pretty Black warmed our lunch. I'll talk to y'all later."

"A'ight, bruh."

"Okay, baby boy. Call back soon when Chinara isn't there, so you can actually pay attention to us."

They laughed and I did, too. That woman had me gone. "Okay. Bye."

"Love you, Haji!"

"Love you, too, Ma."

I ended the call and went to join Chinara at the table. "Your brother is an asshole."

"Yep."

"I'm gonna assume that was Kevin."

"Yep. But enough about them. How yo' poohnani feeling?"

"Good enough to give your anaconda another try."

She sat on the table and spread her legs right next to my food. "Oh, you nasty, girl."

Pulling her t-shirt off, those nipples of hers greeted me, so I went right to them to show them how much I loved them. Swirling my tongue around them, I gently pulled them into my mouth, making love to them, then licked my way to her neck and ear. Scooping her up, I made my way to the bedroom. I would have plunged in her shit raw otherwise. I couldn't wait until the moment that I could.

Once we got to the room, I laid her on the bed and pulled her shorts off, only to see she wasn't wearing underwear. I licked my lips, then slid my hand down my beard. "Did I unleash this in you?" Going to my knees, I asked, "Huh, fat mama? You like what daddy do to you?"

Pushing her legs wider, she moaned loudly as I whispered to her pussy, "I promise to take good care of you today, baby. Damn good care."

I went in, swirling my tongue around my greatest inspiration and slurping up its affection for me as Chinara moaned and grabbed my head. "Hajiii... your head game is unfuckwithable. Shiiiit."

That shit only propelled me forward, sucking that pussy like my life depended on it... like I would die without it. But it was soft, sensual, and tender enough to have her creaming on my lips and in my beard just that quickly. When her hips lifted and her legs had begun trembling, I knew the end was near. Blessing me with all that sweet nectar, I was ready to give her some tender loving.

As I stood, I slid my hands up her long-ass legs. I kissed her calf and gently bit it, then went to the back of her knees. Chinara damn near kicked me. "Oh fuck! What are you doing?"

"Just getting to know your sensitive spots, baby. That cool wit'chu?"

I didn't wait for an answer, just continued to please her and show her things she had no clue about. I kissed, then licked it and made my way to her ankle. These long chocolate legs had my third leg ready for action. Walking around to the nightstand, I got a condom and was quickly about to strap up, but she'd turned over in the bed and grabbed my dick. "What'chu gon' do with it?"

Her eyes lifted to mine as she extended her tongue. After licking the shaft and teasing my balls, she took my dick in my mouth, causing my head to drop back. She was better at it than I thought she would be. Stroking the bottom half of my dick, she sucked the upper half slowly, like she was savoring every moment of this. Moaning on my dick like it was a delicacy, soothing to her palate. Slowly sliding it out of her mouth, I growled, "Fuck!"

Sliding the condom on, I saw her tense up a bit. "Relax, Pretty Black. I promise I'm gon' treat this pussy like porcelain."

She exhaled as she closed her eyes and spread her legs for me. Dropping spit to her pussy, I gently eased the head in. "Oooh, Haji. Yes."

I could feel her body relaxing as I stroked her. My dick was impatient as hell, wanting to be deep in her shit, but I knew what I had to do to get that pussy ready for me. Pushing in a little more, she was still good with that and I stroked her slowly, winding my dick into her as I gradually gave her more. I'd reached the halfway point without problems. That was the furthest I had gone last night before the issues started. Pushing a little past that, I held my position, letting her pussy get acquainted.

After doing that repeatedly, I began long stroking her, feeling her pussy grip me like it was happy I'd come to visit. It didn't want me to leave. I only had about an inch more to get into her before I could be reckless in her shit. "Open your eyes, baby. Let me see your pleasure in them," I said as I gently stroked her.

She slowly opened them staring at me as I filled her repeatedly. "Didn't I tell you I was gon' take care of you?"

"Yes... daddy... shiiiitt!"

I completely filled her and held my position, giving her time to accept all of me. Kissing her ear, then nibbling on her neck, I felt the tension leave her, then I began really long stroking that pussy. Giving her all my technique without hurting her was a relief. My dick was happy as shit now. I picked up my pace some and lifted her leg, letting her knee meet her shoulder. "Oh yeah, Chinara. This my shit forever, baby."

"Haji...yes! Take it! It's yours, baby!"

Her screams and the grip her pussy had on me had me about to cum quicker than I ever had. By far, the best pussy I'd ever had the pleasure of meeting. Turning her to her side, I reentered her, and she screamed, causing me to stop. "Don't stop! Fuck!"

I pushed back inside of her, grateful that it was only her screams of passion. Giving it to her a little more roughly, caused a growl to leave me. I felt like a wild animal attacking its prey, not wanting to let it get away. Turning her again to her stomach, she arched her back perfectly, but I was sure to take it easy at first. "I see why you been keeping this pussy to yourself."

Pulling out, I looked at the creaminess around her entry and wanted to shoot cum all over her ass. I rubbed the head of my latex-covered dick all over it, then pushed back inside of her and slapped her ass. When she began throwing that shit back at me, I knew I could fuck her up. Grabbing her hips, I lit into that pussy like I'd been wanting to since I first saw her. She screamed in ecstasy as she came all over my shaft. I had to slow down to see it coating me and that shit gave me chills. I leaned over her, straddling her legs with mine and fucked her senseless while gripping her hair.

This was the beginning of my insatiable desire for her, so I hoped she was ready to be like this every... fucking... day. Those damn screams had me sensitive as fuck, knowing that I was destroying her pussy so good. "Baby, a nigga 'bout to cum. Fuck!"

"Give... it to... me! Ahh! Haji! I'm cumming, too, daddy!"

She came on me again, some of her juices leaking to the bed. The contracting of her shit took me over the edge. "Fuck!" I growled as I released the most powerful nut known to my body.

Yeah, she was it. Nobody else compared and never would, on my soul.

hinara

I DIDN'T KNOW how I would function in this interview today. Verizon had finally called for a second interview and I couldn't be happier. I didn't tell Haji, because an interview didn't mean I had the job. After I left the shower, I sent him a text. It had become habit to send him a text about ten a.m. just to say, *thinking of you, baby*. It was his first week back in over two weeks, and he'd been worn out. However, he wasn't worn out enough not to kill my shit every night. I'd gotten so adjusted to him until I was begging him to hit me harder. Sometimes that shit brought tears to my eyes, but I was falling for his dick in a major way.

Besides that, he was a gentle soul, the total opposite of what I originally thought about him. I'd only been living with him a week, but it felt like I'd been knowing him for years. His persona was so laidback, I couldn't imagine ever upsetting him again. After getting dressed an entire two hours early, I decided to finally call my family.

My sister didn't have an iPhone, so I couldn't Facetime as Haji had done with his family and my parents didn't have a phone at all. Since my sister still lived there, they believed they were fine without one.

I sent them two hundred dollars, but I didn't think they'd received it just yet. I was still getting unemployment, but I didn't have to spend a dime of it. Haji insisted that I use the card he gave me. As Daraja's phone rang, I silently hoped she would answer. Just before I could hang up, I heard, "Pele o?"

"Hey, sis!"

"Chinara! We missed you so much! What's been up?"

"Well, I met someone that's been taking up quite a bit of my time."

"Oooh," she said, sounding like Megan thee Stallion.

I couldn't help but laugh as she said, "Code for he's been putting it down... blowing the back out... yeah?"

"Hush! Only for like the past week."

"It's about time! He must be really special."

"He's my fiancé, now."

"Oh shit! How long have the two of you known each other?"

"A little over two months, maybe closer to three now."

While I really didn't start getting to know him until a week ago, that was what we told our family since that was when he'd first seen me. "Oh my God! This American man done came in and swept my almost nun-like sister off her feet! Three months, sis!"

I chuckled at her theatrics. "He's not American. I mean, he's a citizen but he isn't from America."

"Where the hell is he from?"

"He's from Sierra Leone."

"You got to be shitting me!"

I laughed loudly as she yelled for my parents. I could hear her practically running through the house. "Nara is engaged! And get this! Her fiancé is from Salone!"

I could hear my mama screaming in excitement, but my dad was extremely quiet. "Hi, Mama. Hi, Daddy."

"Chinara! Engaged? I can't believe it! Congratulations, baby!"

"Thank you, Mama."

"Hello, daughter. How is your career going?"

"Not too good, Daddy. That's why I haven't called much. I didn't want you to worry. I'm receiving unemployment benefits, but I have a job interview today. The radio station laid me off two months ago. But I'm grateful for Haji, because he stepped up at a time in my life where I didn't know what to do."

"What does he do for work?" my dad asked sternly.

"He's a chemical engineer, Papa."

"I want to be happy for you, daughter, but all I can think about is your heart. After Kemweh breaking you, I've gotten more protective of you. How does he treat you?"

"Like a queen... a precious jewel. I feel cherished, Papa. Something I've never felt by a man. When I see him, my heart melts every time."

"That's what I want to hear. I wish you could come home, even if it's just to visit. These ten years have been hard, Chi Chi."

My heart sank to my feet. Whenever my dad called me Chi Chi, it made me sensitive, because I knew that was how he was feeling. "Maybe I can come visit soon. I'll talk to Haji about it."

"Just the fact that it's something you can talk to him about, makes me feel a little more relaxed. I love you, doll."

"I love you, too. Haji calls me his pretty black doll. So, you two have that in common."

I heard him chuckle and that made me feel better. "Okay. Here's your mama."

"Just the sound of your voice when you talk about him lets me know that he's doing *everything* right," she said, then she and Daraja died in laughter.

I couldn't help but join them. There was no point in denying it. "Yes. Everything."

"Okay, okay. Bring it to another room," Papa said.

They laughed more as I heard them moving. "Send us a picture of him, Nara!"

"I will, but you better not be fantasizing about my man."

We laughed more as I sent the picture. As I did, a text came through from him. *You're always on my mind, Pretty Black Doll.* I smiled and somewhat got lost in his text as I heard, "Oh shit! He's fine, Nara!"

I rolled my eyes as my mama said, "Let me see, girl. You're hogging the phone."

She was quiet for a second, then she said, "Oh. Okay. Sierra Leone, huh? He looks as American as they get."

"He's been here for fourteen years and kind of has a sour taste in his mouth about home because of his family."

"Oh. That's no good. But he's very handsome. As long as he's good to you, that's all I'm worried about."

"How's your health, Mama?"

"It's been good. We were a little low on money for my medication, but your uncle loaned us some money."

"I sent two hundred dollars to you guys. That should help significantly."

"Two hundred dollars? That's a lot of money!"

I smiled. Two hundred dollars in Nigeria would get them a long way. Two hundred dollars to them was like having two thousand to an American. But the amount of money I sent them was 77,500 Nigerian Naira. They could buy necessities and save some money for rough days. "Make sure to take care of yourself. I love you guys, but I have to go. I need to eat breakfast and then go to my interview."

"Okay, Nara. We love you! Don't wait so long to call us again."

"I won't. Hopefully, I'll be able to call again next week. And I love you all, too."

I ended the call amidst their goodbyes, then headed to the kitchen. After putting a bagel in the toaster, I finally updated my social media pages, officially taking myself off the market. I didn't want to update it before talking to my family. Had Daraja seen that on Facebook before I told them, she would have gone ballistic on me when I would have called.

After eating and drinking some tea, I headed to Verizon to interview with the hiring supervisor. I was somewhat nervous, but I knew there was no reason they should pass me up for the position... well, unless I was overqualified. I'd heard that word quite a bit in my job hunt. I'd been denied by all of the other retail outlets. Hopefully, that wouldn't be the case here.

When I got there, after letting someone know I was there for the interview, I sat in the front. I was a whole fifteen minutes early. It was always better to be early than late. That way people knew that you took the interview seriously. After about ten minutes, the lady I remembered as Kyley came out with another lady to get me. Following them to the office, Kyley gave me a slight smirk that made me somewhat uncomfortable. "Hello, Ms..."

"Why-choo-koo."

"I apologize. I'm Gloria Tatum. Kyley recommended you for this interview and as I looked over your resume, I realized you would be a great hire... just not for a sales associate. There's a position in marketing that's open and if you're okay with that, I would love to refer you to their department."

My eyebrows went up slightly as Kyley frowned. I bet that was a position she wanted or had applied for. "Sure. That's great. Thank you. Is that department here?"

"It's in Houston actually."

I thought about what Haji told me about the house his father left him in Houston and thought it would be perfect. Driving back and forth for the next six to eight months would be taxing, but it would be worth it. "Okay. That's great."

She smiled at me and wrote something on a sheet of paper, then scanned the documents and emailed them to a supervisor while Kyley stared me down. I didn't like her ass and I didn't know what her problem was with me suddenly. She seemed somewhat fake for my first interview, but it wasn't something that really bothered me.

But the way she was behaving now was making me uncomfortable as hell. However, I wasn't the type to let anyone intimidate me. She could catch me outside and we could settle this today. My education level didn't dictate my personality. I could get just as ignorant. I didn't have a problem going to the gutter and checking her ass.

Ms. Tatum looked up at me and gave me contact information for a man named Howard Lomax. "He's the supervisor. If you haven't heard from him by the end of next week, give him a call."

"Yes, ma'am. Thank you so much."

She nodded and I stood from my seat, then stared at Kyley. I slightly rolled my eyes as I exited the office. Before I could get to the door, I noticed she was behind me. When I turned to confront her, she said, "Congratulations on the upgrade."

I frowned, allowing my eyes to narrow. "You got a problem with me? I don't even know you."

She smacked her lips as I walked out the door and said, "I do. First of all, that position was supposed to be for in-house applicants first before it was opened to the public. Secondly, I been fucking your fiancé, but he has the nerve to wanna marry you. You ain't got shit on me."

It dawned on me that she was the one Haji had probably fucked that night we got into it. Our relationship was none of her business. She was assuming that Haji had cheated on me with her. That wasn't the case. We didn't confirm what was up with us until the next day. "I have plenty on you, because first, I know how to be a respectable woman and not a disrespectful slut. Your problem should be with him, not me. To approach a woman about her fiancé is not only disrespectful, but it's ratchet. It's ghetto and hoe-ish. Although I have an amazing education and I seem prim and proper, I would suggest you not run up on me again. I will dip down to the slums where you are and fuck you up, especially when it comes to Haji."

I walked away from her before I slapped the shit out of her. My temperament was usually level, but she had me angry enough to lose my dignity for a second. The shocked look on her face was just the expression I liked to see when I had to get at somebody. It wasn't often I had to do that, but it had happened with my last boyfriend a couple of times within the year we dated. People took my friendly demeanor to mean I would let them get away with shit. Not the case.

As I headed back to the house, my anger hadn't subsided. I was still somewhat upset with Haji. He knew I had interviewed there. He'd seen me. But he still had the nerve to go fuck that girl after I was living here. What if they would have hired me as a sales associate? That bitch would have been my supervisor and we would have had problems. Major problems. Doing my best to cool off, I turned on some music by Sammie. He was my bae in my mind. Maybe he could help me calm down before my real-life bae got off work.

Once I got home, I started cooking a fish and yam stew. It was an easy Nigerian dish that wouldn't take long to cook. Most people from West and South Africa were familiar with the dish. Within an hour or two, I was done. Going upstairs to lay across the bed, my mind went back to that bitch and I couldn't help but text Haji. *Is Kyley one of the bitches you were fucking?*

My mind wouldn't let me rest about the issue without saying something immediately. My phone chimed and I quickly snatched it up from the bed. *Yes.*

That was it. That was all he had to say. At least he didn't lie. But my anger was only growing at this point. It was only lunchtime and Haji didn't get off until six. *That's it? That's all you have to say?*

I stood from the bed and paced back and forth across the room, trying to calm down. He was at work and I was fucking up his day. But whatever, because my day was fucked up. She probably saw our picture on his Facebook page or any other social media pages they were connected on. Stupid hoe. My phone chimed and I looked at his nonchalant-ass text message. *We'll talk about it when I get home, Pretty Black. Have you a drink and relax for me.*

If that wasn't some playboy shit, I didn't know what was. But my ass was gon' definitely have a drink. Going downstairs I rummaged through the liquor cabinet to find a bottle of Captain Morgan Spiced

Rum. Oh, I was about to get fucked up. It was so smooth tasting. I took a swig straight from the bottle, then headed to the couch and turned on the TV, the bottle still in my hand. Turning the channel to find *Sanford and Son*, I continued to drink. As my body heated up, I started shedding clothes until I was in my bra and thong. When I realized I'd drank the entire bottle, I decided to take a nap before I got sick.

aji

"Pretty Black. Wake up, baby," I said as I took my shirt off.

Baby girl was passed out on the couch. Her titties were hanging out of her bra and her pussy was eating the fuck out of the thong she was wearing. I'd gone straight upstairs and took a shower when I saw her lying there, looking like she was ready to be taken advantage of. After coming out of my sweats, letting my dick hang, I tried to wake her up again, but she didn't budge. Grabbing the condom from the table, I slid it on, then got on my knees, turned her body, and pulled that thong off. I had something to wake that ass up.

Her pussy was so wet. That was that drunken horniness and I couldn't wait to see how nasty she would get. Putting her legs on my shoulders, I entered her and stroked that shit slow, watching my entry and departure. Letting it slide all the way out, hearing a slight noise when I did, only turned me on more. She was still out but moaning in her drunkenness. Sliding back inside of her, I pulled out again. She lifted her hand as her legs fell from my shoulders. "Hajiii," she moaned. "Who you fucking?"

"I'm fucking my wife-to-be. The best pussy I ever had. Fuck those other hoes."

Her eyes opened slowly as I pushed back inside of her. "Why you fucked that bitch when you knew I was trying to get a job there?"

"I was fucking her ass before that. She was just somebody I knew I could get one off with."

I began fucking her harder as she tried to get away. "No. Fuck this! That was selfish and thoughtless. What if I have to work with her?"

"You don't have to work at all. Now quit running from this dick. You know you want it. That pussy sopping wet," I said as she rolled over to her stomach.

Grabbing her roughly, I pulled her ass to me and plunged in her pussy, making her cum all over my dick as she screamed. Dropping spit on her asshole, I pushed a finger into it as I fucked her. It was clinching my finger like it wanted me there and that shit was threatening to take me out the game. "You like me penetrating that asshole, baby?"

"Oh yes! Fuck me, Haji! Pleeeaaase...."

Sliding my finger in and out of her anus, I could feel the head of my dick through the layer of skin and tissue separating the two. What caught me off-guard was the sudden wetness of her asshole. I pulled my finger out to see that she'd had an anal orgasm. "Oh, you a nasty-ass freak, huh?"

"You like it... 'cause you a nasty muthafucka, too. Shit!"

"Mmm-hmm. Give me that shit."

"You just make sure... I don't have to fuck nobody up... about what's mine."

"Naw... I can't have my pretty, black doll scrapping in these streets. You too queenly for that shit."

"Then check her ass so I don't have to."

With that, she started throwing that ass back for a real nigga. I remained still for a moment and watched her groove on my shit, then slapped her ass cheeks one at a time. Grabbing a hold of her hips, I began slamming into her, bringing her orgasm to the surface. "You in here drinking up my good shit over a bitch that don't mean nothing to me. I'm 'bout to fuck the lining out yo' pussy."

She screamed as I plummeted her repeatedly but made love to her at the same time. Words failed her and once my nut surfaced, words failed me, too. Lying on top of her as my dick rested inside of her, I kissed her back, then her neck. Feeling her clammy skin against my wet skin was an aphrodisiac for me. Sliding out of her, I went straight up on my knees and rolled her over. I lifted her legs and commenced to eating the fuck out of her pussy. Sprung wasn't the word to describe just how much I needed her. Addiction was real and just that quickly, she had me strung out.

She was so worn out and her pussy had been contracting so much, she could barely voice her satisfaction. She'd experienced an overload already and I loved the way her body couldn't help but respond to me. As her tremors took over her, she looked like she wanted to cry. When the wave subsided, I stood to my feet and picked her up, cradling her like the precious possession she was. I didn't know how she would make it through a shower or bath because she was tore the fuck up. I guess I would have to take care of her tonight... but that was nothing new. Taking care of her was my mission in life... to eventually fall in love with her.

I was thankful that it was the weekend because I was tired as hell. That week back at work wore me out. Keeping my queen satisfied had been a task as well. I'd awakened the beast in her ass and now she wanted it all the damn time. Thankfully, she wasn't throwing up once that liquor wore off. But she woke up at like midnight and straddled me. She'd put the condom on and everything and rode my dick like it was taking her somewhere. I supposed it took her exactly where she wanted to go because once the ride was over, she fell off my shit and went right back to sleep.

This morning I woke up to waffles, eggs, and bacon. I was still sluggish, though. I knew I wouldn't be doing shit today. I'd planned to go work out with Jarius later, but we would see. I was sitting on the couch with my feet up, full as hell. Chinara had gone to the sunroom to relax and read. It might have been a bad time, but I decided to squash this shit right now with Kyley. Going to my contacts in my phone, I called her. I didn't know if she had to work today or not. If she was at work, she wouldn't answer. But apparently, she was off, because she answered, "Hey, daddy. You need a tune-up?"

"Hell naw. What I need is for you to back up off my fiancée. Savor that shit you got last Friday because it won't happen again. However you found out who she was is of no consequence. But keep your words, your eyeballs, and your hands to your fucking self. I don't have a problem digging up my roots and treating you like the African men of olden times. That woman, Chinara, is who I want. She's who I need. You clinging on to something you never really had. Get over that shit and move on wit'cho life before I have to help you move on."

"Well, fuck you, too! African bitch."

She ended the call and I smirked, feeling pleased with myself. Sensing someone was watching me, I turned my head to look behind me and saw Chinara standing there with her hand on her chest. "What's up, baby? You a'ight?"

"Yeah. Just hearing you check her made me horny."

I rolled my eyes playfully as she continued. "But you also have this that came in the mail."

Looking at the envelope, I couldn't make out what it was, but when she put it in my hands, I knew it was the results of my blood test. "You already gave me the pussy, though. So, I guess this really doesn't matter."

"It doesn't matter if wanna keep wearing condoms and if you never want me to swallow your cum."

I tore that letter open so fast. Ain't no way I wanted to go another day without feeling that pussy raw. *And* she wanted to swallow my babies? Shiiiid. A nigga scanned through that letter fast as hell to see that I was negative for every test they put my blood through. I gave the letter to her and pulled my shorts off sitting right there on the couch, letting my dick bounce right out of that shit. She laughed as she stared at me. "Well, I guess you don't wanna waste any time, huh?"

I laughed, too, then said, "I'm clowning, girl, but later, I'm gon' want that pussy bust wide open for me."

"That isn't an issue and you know that. She's always ready for you."

I slapped her ass as she walked away to the kitchen, then pulled my shorts up. I was surprised she walked away from all this dick. Although I was tired, I would have blessed her ass with all these inches wherever she wanted them. And since she'd said she was horny, I knew she should have been ready to hop on it. Deciding not to let her be, I got up and went to the sunroom to see her typing feverishly in her phone. "What's up? You looked pissed."

She exhaled loudly, then handed me her phone. It was a message from Kevin. Looking closer, I saw the message had come through on Instagram. *I don't know what you're up to, but I'm going to be checking into you and my no-good brother. This feels like a setup.*

I dropped her phone in her lap and went back up front to grab my cell phone, calling him immediately. "I guess she's with you."

"Listen and listen good. What I do is my fucking business. My wife-to-be is none of your concern. For you to message her through IG, that's fucking pussy moves. No matter what you think about what we have going on, we know what's between us. It ain't for nobody else to know. Message her again and I'm gon' make some moves all the way from Texas on yo' ass. I'm sicka yo' ass, nigga."

"Whatever. I think you just tryna marry somebody for that money."

"Muthafucka, even if that was the case, it's my fucking money. I have every right to that shit and if I wanted to be a nigga about it, I'd contest those stipulations in court. So, fuck you and any other mutha-fucka that got some shit to say. Stay the fuck away from my woman's inbox!"

I ended the call and walked back to the sunroom and pulled Chinara from the rocking chair she was seated in. "Fuck him. Block him on your social media."

"I will. Why is he this way?"

"I don't know. It's like we've been in competition our whole lives. I think he wanted to do all the things I did but didn't. Of course, that ain't a justifiable reason for him to be the way he is, but that's what I think. I'm sorry that he got at'chu like that. I gave him a good cussing over the phone."

"I heard. Do you think he feels you got more attention?"

"I don't know. I definitely got more negative attention, always getting fussed at by my father. Kevin was doing the same shit I was doing, but I was just the one that didn't feel the need to sneak around. I was the rebellious one. Hence the reason the two of them got their inheritance and I didn't."

"Well, don't concentrate on that. I got other shit for you to concentrate on."

"You know, since you been around me, your mouth has gotten extremely dirty. Am I a bad influence on you?"

She giggled, then looked up at me. "It was always there. You just unlocked it. It had been locked away for so long, I'd forgotten it was there."

Sliding her hand down my chest, she made her way to my erection. "Besides, I think since I checked your brother, my temper has calmed down enough to feel that raw dick inside of me. What do you think?"

"You saw the message before you brought me the mail?"

"While you were busy tearing the envelope open, he sent the message. Enough of that. You want this shit or not?" she asked as she stroked my dick through the shorts I wore.

"You know I will dig in that gushy shit anywhere. But this

moment is going to be monumental. No latex. But you know what I wanna do?"

"What?"

"After careful consideration, I don't think I wanna experience you raw until you marry me."

Her eyebrows lifted slightly. "But... I mean... what will the difference be? We don't even know what will come out of it. We're just going with the flow for now."

"I know what's gonna come out of it, Pretty Black. You should know, too. We get along far too well for this to end. Plus, that fat muthafucka got a hold on me. I'm not letting go, Chinara."

"So... are you saying this marriage is really real? We've only known one another for a week."

"That's where you wrong. I been knowing you for a couple of months. I watched you when you didn't know I was watching you."

Sliding her strap off her shoulder, I continued. "Every curve your body took was branded in my mental. The way your eyes show your true emotions intrigues me. How you pop your hip out when you're about to speak matter of fact-ly, is sexy as hell. How your ears sometime lift slightly when you frown, lets me know that you're more curious at that moment than angry."

Pulling the tank down over her nipples, I lowered my head and gently sucked one. Her hands went to the sides of my head and she moaned as my hands slid up her thighs. Those wind shorts were about to come off and I was ready to take her to ecstasy, until she whispered, "Stop, Haji."

 hinara

His brows furrowed as I pulled up my tank top and stepped away from him. My sex was throbbing and cursing me out for denying her, but if he was taking this marriage seriously, there were things I wanted to do. "Haji... since you're taking this even more seriously than I thought, maybe we should take a step back from sex until we're married."

He frowned harder. "Why? We already fucking. What's the point in stopping?"

"I just thought that it would be more emotion-filled if we stopped."

He lifted me by grabbing ahold of my thighs. "Hell naw. I ain't stopping shit. Not dipping into you raw is as far as I wanna go. You ain't finna deprive me of my good shit altogether. Hell naw."

He began making his way up the stairs as he threw me over his shoulder, making me giggle. As we ascended, his phone rang. Once we got to the top, he set me on my feet and checked it. "Fuck. That's my job."

He stepped away from me and answered the phone. There was a slight panic in his facial expression that put me on edge as he listened. "Shit. Okay."

When he ended the call, he said, "Well, that pussy gets to make it another day. I gotta go to work... there was a small chemical spill, but a couple of guys have to go get checked out."

"Do you know how long you'll be gone?"

"No, baby. I won't know until I get there."

"Okay."

He walked into the bedroom and got his Nomex, then kissed my lips and headed out. I didn't know what I was going to do now to help pass the time. Going back to the sunroom, I decided to go back to reading a new book by India T. Norfleet. I didn't know why I wanted to continue the book, since Haji had left. That was what had me horny in the first place. The story was intriguing though, so I decided I would continue torturing myself.

As I read the freaky-ass love scene I was on, my phone rang, interrupting my reading time. It was Donovan. He hadn't tried to call in a while. "Hello?"

"Chinara! You finally answered! How are you?"

"I'm doing okay, Donovan. How are you?"

"I'm good. I didn't know what had happened to you. I'd gone by your place a week ago and someone else greeted me at the door. You sure you okay?"

"Yeah, I'm good. I still don't have a job and I got evicted, but I moved in with my fiancé."

"Fiancé? Wow. I didn't know you were involved with anyone."

"We've moved kind of fast in our relationship. We met the exact same day I got laid off. So, I'm just thankful that God sent him at a time that I needed him."

"You know I was down to help you, though."

"I know. And I appreciate that Donovan. I was okay that first month. After that, it went downhill fast. My unemployment didn't kick in right away of course, so it was hell trying to play catch up."

"Well... is he treating you right?"

I could hear the disappointment in his voice. Donovan wouldn't be a bad catch if he would handle that body odor. Of course, he was nowhere near Haji in comparison, but he was nice-looking. I wasn't attracted to him in no way, though. He was a great co-worker and was a good friend. That was it. "He treats me very well, Donovan. Thanks."

"Okay. Well, I heard that 102.5 was hiring if you're interested."

"Okay. I'll shoot my resume to them. I have a pending interview with Verizon in their marketing department as well."

"That's great. Is that in Beaumont?"

"No. Houston. I'll have to drive back and forth until Haji can get situated with a job out there as well. Well... that's if I get the job."

"I don't see why you wouldn't. You're extremely smart and dedicated. Any business would benefit by having you on their team."

"That's really nice of you, Donovan. Thank you."

"Are you busy? You wanna meet for lunch?"

"No, I better not. I had a late breakfast, so I'm not really hungry."

"Aww, come on, Nara. Your fiancé can come, too. I just wanna see my friend."

He seemed a little pushy and that seemed suspicious to me. I didn't like that feeling. It wasn't like we went to lunch together all the time. We'd only gone to lunch once the entire time we'd known one another, and two other co-workers had joined us. So, his behavior was somewhat weird. "No. That would be awkward. Just Facetime me."

"A'ight. That's cool."

He switched the call to a Facetime and once I answered, the excitement shown in his eyes. I smiled and I saw a flash. "Did you just take a picture of me?"

"Yeah. You look beautiful. That way I can see you when I want. This may be our last time talking."

I rolled my eyes playfully, but I was still a little uneasy about what had just happened. I was already regretting letting him Face-time me. "So, how are things at the station?"

"They're okay. It hadn't really been the same without you, Janelle, and Adrianne, but it hadn't been horrible either."

"Well, I guess that's good."

I still felt weirded out by the way he was staring at me. "You are so beautiful, Chinara. Your pretty, chocolate skin seems to be glowing."

"It's glowing because I'm extremely happy, Donovan. I have to go," I said with a frown, then snapped a picture of my own.

"I didn't mean to offend you. I was just making an observation. I'll let you go. Hopefully, I'll see you soon. If not, take care of yourself."

"Bye."

That was the weirdest shit ever. I went back to my book and just as I read about how the man in the story was manhandling the female character against a wall, Haji sent a message. *I miss you already Pretty Black. I should be home in a couple of hours.*

I exhaled with a smile. Being here all day without him and not having close friends was a drag. I knew quite a few people, but I was never one to go out, so I didn't develop those types of relationships. I went to restaurants and that was about it. A couple of times I'd gone bowling with a group of people, but I didn't really enjoy it that much. That was probably because Donovan's stank ass was there. He always insisted on putting his arm around me. Sometimes he would be so ripe, I would have to go to the bathroom or somewhere away from him to keep from throwing up.

Not having a job made me become more acquainted with myself, and I was appreciative for that time. It made me realize that while I didn't have close friends, I really didn't enjoy being alone that much. When I had a job, it was different. I only had to be alone with myself for a few hours. But after a week of being in Haji's home, I knew I really didn't like being here without him. His days at work this past week, I'd gotten my things organized and gon' to the store to make the room feel like home, but that was unnecessary since I'd been sleeping with him.

Going to the room to put on a bra and some pants, I decided to go to the store to get some plantains to go with the stew I'd cooked yesterday. I could fry them as a side. We had enough left for a late lunch. Taking the time to text Haji back, I typed, *I miss you, too. I'm going to the store for plantains. Do you need anything?*

By the time I'd made it down the stairs, he'd texted back, *Honey and chocolate syrup. Oh, and a can of whipped cream.*

My face heated up as I shook my head slowly. He was so damn nasty, and I loved it. I quickly texted him back as I grabbed my keys and asked, *What are you gonna do with that?*

Getting in my car, I headed to the grocery store, waiting for Haji's nasty-ass response, but it never came. I figured he'd gotten busy. That happened quite a bit when we were texting while he was working. After getting the plantains and picking up the items he'd asked for, I made my way back to the house. Once I peeled them and cut them, I added a little oil to the skillet and put them in, sprinkling a little sea salt to bring out the flavor.

The whole process only took about fifteen to twenty minutes. Grabbing one from the plate I put them on, I popped it in my mouth. Closing my eyes as I chewed it, I was tempted to eat all of them. They were so good, and it had been a while since I'd had any. They always reminded me of my aunt because she loved them. Smiling slightly at her memory, my phone chimed with a Facebook notification. When I grabbed my phone to look at it, I nearly lost my damn mind. Donovan had posted that fucking picture he took of me, saying one day I would be his. Not only did he tag me in it, but he tagged Haji.

My entire body heated up in anger. I commented on his photo with the picture I snapped and asked, *What in the fuck is your motive?*

Why would he do some shit like that? I would have never accused him of being petty and shady like that. That may have been why Haji hadn't responded to me. I noticed he made the post almost an hour ago, but for some reason, I was just getting notified of it. I immediately texted Haji. *Everything okay, baby?*

I didn't want to alert him of the post if he hadn't seen it yet. Telling him some bullshit like that on his job was a no-no. I'd done that shit last time, and I'd regretted it. I wouldn't want to be arguing with my significant other while I was at work. My phone chimed and the message said, *We'll talk when I get home.*

That let me know that he'd seen it. He had to know that I wouldn't fuck around on him. When he first slid inside of me, he knew I wasn't lying about my celibacy. I wouldn't even think about seeing someone else. I wanted to call Donovan, but instead, I chose to block him. Calling him would only make the situation worse. I was so nervous about what Haji would say or do. He would probably be here in less than an hour now.

After wrapping up the plantains, I took the stew from the fridge and set it on the stove. I'd heat it up whenever he was ready to eat. Walking up the stairs, I felt like I'd fucked up. I shouldn't have let him Facetime me. That was so stupid. When I got to the room, I flopped to the bed, instantly smelling Haji's beard oil. Falling to my back, I laid there until I heard the back door open and his keys hit the countertop. I took a deep breath and kept my eyes closed tight until he opened the door.

I sat up and looked at him. He didn't look angry or upset, but I still kept my mouth closed. He got undressed, then turned to me and said, "We'll talk after I get out the shower."

I nodded. He was so calm, and that shit had me trembling. I'd never really seen him angry and I didn't know what to expect. I'd heard him mouth off to Kyley and his brother, but that shit wasn't directed at me. If his brother saw it, this would only give him ammunition against him. *Ugh!* I stood from the bed and he stepped out of the bathroom, naked as the day he was born and walked over to me. Grabbing my hand, he pulled me to the bathroom. Gently sliding my tank top off, he stared into my eyes as his hands traveled behind me to unfasten my bra. The tremble going through my body didn't go unnoticed by him.

Lowering my head, cowering in his presence, he lifted it by my chin. "What did I tell you about doing that shit?"

His lips went to my neck as he tilted my head back and his hands slid to my waistband, pulling my pants and undergarments off. Sliding my tank down my body as well, he stared at my nakedness, taking in every inch of me. He pulled my hair up and tied it up with one of my scrunchies from the vanity, then led me to the shower. No words were spoken as he went to his knees, kissing my stomach, sides, and lastly my mound. I didn't know how to react to his tenderness.

Standing to soap my loofah, he began washing my body. Instead of turning me around to wash my back, he pulled me closed to him. My nipples were hard enough to cut glass as they pressed into his ribcage. *How could I be horny and nervous at the same damn time?* I laid my head against his shoulder as he washed my back and neck. Pulling away from me, he went to his knees again and began washing my lower extremities, sending bolts of electricity through my body.

Once he was done washing me, he stood like the commander and chief of an army. His presence screamed respect, power, and authority. I began washing him as he'd done me, but I refused to look into his eyes. I couldn't handle it. After I'd washed every part of him, lingering on his dick for a while, I finally gathered the courage to face him. He'd been staring at me almost the entire time. His gaze was like an all-consuming fire. Everything about me screamed Haji.

After rinsing off the soap, he backed me into the corner and lifted me. I already knew what was to follow. He'd said to hell with not feeling me raw until we were married. Maybe he was only going to be married to me for the amount of time specified now, but I was dying to know what he was thinking. However, those thoughts were out of my mind as soon as he slid his dick into me. My head dropped back to the wall and a soft moan left my lips. Feeling him buried deep inside of me, without anything between us was like heaven.

When I opened my eyes to look at him, I knew he was about to put me through hell. He had a slight frown on his face when he thrust into me, causing me to scream out in ecstasy. "Who is he?"

Before I could answer, his fingers dug into my skin as he fucked me hard. "Who the fuck is he, Chinara?"

"My ex-co-worker. He called to check on me."

Grabbing my nipple with his teeth, I yelped in excitement, excreting the cream he loved so much on his dick. "If he called, why were y'all Facetiming?"

"He wanted to take me to lunch and I declined. So, I allowed him to Facetime me. Oh shit! Haji!"

He hadn't let up. He was killing my pussy as I held on tightly to him, lowering my head to his neck and biting him like I was a fucking vampire. He growled out as he dug deeper inside of me, squeezing the life out of my ass. "You shouldn't have Facetimed him."

"I know, but I had no idea... fuck! I had no idea he would do something like that. Haji... please forgive me, baby. I don't know why he did that."

He didn't respond to me, just continued to assault my senses and my pussy. His aura had filled the shower and it felt like I was about to suffocate in it. Suddenly, he slowed down and asked, "You obviously mean something to him. Does he mean anything to you?"

"No. I hadn't spoken to him since my last day at the station. You are the only man I care about. I promise... I belong to you, Haji. Only you."

He began his assault again, causing my screams to echo off the shower walls as I held on for dear life. My chocolate skin was gaining a red hue from the hot water and passion that he filled me with. In a short amount of time, Haji was my everything, and losing him frightened me. It wasn't just because he was taking care of me, but the way in which he cherished me kept me longing for him. The fuckboy I thought he was, was clearly a misconception and a terribly wrong assumption. Haji was all man with the woman that was for him. "Since you belong to me, I want that bitch unfriended on social media."

"Already done and blocked."

"And also, since you're mine, I need you to open your heart and freefall with me. Don't worry about shit... just me and you."

"Gladly, Haji."

"Lastly, I need you to cum on daddy dick, 'cause I'm about to pump you with some premium shit."

"Hajiii... oluwa mi o! Jowo!"

My body felt like it was exploding all over him as I bucked against him, giving him everything he deserved. My pleas in my native tribal language didn't go unnoticed as he dug into me. "Oh fuck!" he growled. As he panted against my neck, he whispered, "Du yaa noh lehf mi."

The tears fell down my cheeks as I listened to him beg me not to leave him. I didn't even think he meant to say that aloud. At that moment, he seemed like a little boy that craved love and affection. "Haji, I will never leave you, baby. We're freefalling, remember?"

He lifted his head and looked into my eyes. "I'm falling for real, Pretty Black."

Pulling his head back to my chest, I said, "You aren't alone, baby. You aren't alone."

Haji

SEEING that picture of my pretty black doll on Facebook in a face-time call with that desperate muthafucka had me seething with anger. But the moment I got home and saw her, I was scared. I supposed the whole reason I hadn't allowed myself to fall for anybody was because I was scared. I didn't come to that conclusion until Saturday. While I had been convinced that I just wasn't ready, that moment showed me otherwise. I was falling hard for my pretty black doll and there was nothing I could do to stop it or slow it down.

For my lunch break, Chinara and I had gone to the courthouse and applied for our marriage license. Friday we would be at the courthouse to get married. As we signed our names, I'd stared at her, feeling that this moment was something I would cherish forever. I knew from the moment I saw her that she was the one, but I had no idea I would feel this way. That it would happen this fast. She pulled out my innermost feelings, causing me to admit all kinds of shit I would have kept to myself.

As we left the courthouse hand in hand, I smiled at her. "So, what are you going to do for the rest of your day?"

"Wait for you to come back to me. I already cooked and straightened up the house."

"I'm gonna book us a flight to Lagos. I know you miss your family. Instead of a honeymoon, we can go see what we can do to help your people."

She turned to me, her eyes wide, and jumped into my arms. "I told my daddy that I would ask if we could go, but after that shit with Donovan, I forgot all about it. I haven't seen them in ten years."

"That's far too long, Chinara. Let me see when I can take more vacation and we'll go. Secondly... this job with Verizon. How badly do you want it?"

She shrugged her shoulders. "It depends on what they offer as far as pay and benefits."

"You know you don't have to work. It's my job to take care of and provide for you. Getting married is a qualifying event for health insurance. I can add you to mine at work. As far as money, I make six figures a year. Now if you're just in love with your career path, I don't have a problem with you working. I would still prefer treating you like a queen. Let me keep your pretty ass like you need to be kept."

She lowered her head, and I hated that she did that. It always reminded me of the chauvinistic ways of the men in my family. "Please lift your head, baby."

"I'm sorry. It's just the way I show you my respect and submission. I'm honoring you as my king when I do that."

"I appreciate that, baby. But you can honor me in other ways. I don't like it. It makes it seem like you're my subordinate."

When we got to her car, I leaned against it and she rested her palm on my cheek. "I'll try to remember that. Old habits die hard. Please be patient with me."

Lowering my head to hers, I kissed her pretty lips, sucking her bottom one into my mouth. Roughly pulling her hips to me, I almost got carried away right outside in the courthouse parking lot. "I will, Pretty Black. I can't wait to spoil you."

I took her saying she was submitting to me to mean that she wouldn't be pursuing the job. If that was the case, I would be sure to forever show her my devotion to her. There wouldn't be anything or anyone that was worth more than her. She smiled at me, then got in her car. "See you in a few hours, Haji."

"A'ight, baby."

I went to my Range and watched her drive away. This time Friday, I would be a married man and that shit felt better than I could have ever imagined it would. As I drove back to work, my phone rang. Lately, when my phone rang, if it wasn't Chinara, I expected the damn worse. Ever since this foolish shit my father had done, it was one thing after the next. I could honestly say that I resented everything about him. Answering the call from my mother, I said, "Hello?"

"Haji! Kusheh!"

"Hey, Mama."

"How's everything? Are you still on your lunch break?"

"Yes. I'm on my way back to work now."

"Umaru told me about the difficulties you've been having with Kevin. I spoke to him and I'm sorry that he feels the need to critique everything you do."

"I handled it, Ma. You don't have to apologize for a grown man."

"But he's a product of me and your father, so I feel somewhat responsible. How are things with Chinara? Did I remember her name correctly?"

"That's it, Ma. Things are great. We actually applied for our marriage license today. There's no point in prolonging the inevitable."

"Wow. So, when are you getting married?"

"Friday."

"Haji. Really? You don't want me there?"

"I didn't think you would come. I've been here fourteen years and you haven't visited."

She was quiet for a moment, then she changed the subject. "Well... I hope you are planning to give me grandbabies sometime in the future."

"I don't know. I'm good either way."

"Okay, son. Well, I'll let you enjoy the rest of your lunchtime. Call me soon."

"Okay."

"I love you."

"I love you, too."

Ending the call, I was hoping she would have said that since Dad was gone that things had changed. I wasn't so lucky. Maybe his beliefs were hers as well. Whatever the case, it wouldn't stop me from making Chinara my wife.

JARIUS and I sat on my patio as he cut my hair. I couldn't make it to the shop and tomorrow was the big day. Surprisingly, my nerves were still calm. Chinara was still at the beautician and she said that I couldn't see her tonight. I didn't know how that was supposed to go down when we lived together, but I would do my best to honor her wishes. This whole situation was crazy. What started out as somewhat of a business proposal had become a life guarantee. I was willing to build a future with a woman who I'd only first seen three months ago. "You nervous about tomorrow?" Jarius asked.

"Not at all. I feel at ease, surprisingly. This is more than I originally thought it would be, bruh. I have feelings for Chinara. I think I love her."

"You think? Ain't no question about that shit. When she's around, you can't focus on shit else."

"Shut up."

"Did you see yourself two weekends ago for the boil? We couldn't effectively talk to you and expect a response until Pretty Black went in the house."

"Aye, nigga. What I tell you about that shit? I'm the only muthafucka gon' call her that."

He chuckled. I knew he did that shit on purpose just to get a rise out of me. "Whatever. She had any mo' problems with that nigga on Facebook?"

"Not that I know of. I felt like a weak-ass nigga with that shit."

"What'chu mean?"

"In the back of my mind, I didn't think she would do no shit like that to me. But instead of being pissed and wanting to get at that nigga, all I could think about was what I would do if she left me."

"And you *think* you in love. Man, get the fuck outta here. I never in my life thought I'd be even having this type of conversation with you. That woman has changed the hell out of you and for the better. I mean, she changed your way with women, because you still the same jackass with me."

"That ain't gon' change, because you still the same muthafucka that like to talk shit."

"All I know is that you need to give me my props. It was my idea for you to ask her to marry you in the first place."

I rolled my eyes and I knew I was never gonna hear the end of that shit. Approaching Chinara about that shit had never crossed my mind. I was just gonna let the money sit there. All the money he'd sent me over the years while I was in school had drawn a nice amount of interest. The Sierra Leonean leone wasn't shit compared to the US dollar, but a lot of the people he did business with paid him in US dollars. So, when I got money from him, I sat it in an account. Not only that, but I worked during school. I was always responsible when it came to money. Tricking it off never crossed my mind.

So, if I never got my inheritance, in my mind, I was like, *fuck it*. However, that was rightfully my money. And I could have gone the route of going to court to get it. That shit only made my heart harder towards my dad. It was always in my mind to pursue something with

Chinara, but not to move it along this fast. Had she not been in the predicament she was in, she probably wouldn't have agreed to it. So, we would both benefit from this arrangement sooner than later.

As Jarius stood in front of me, tightening up my edge, I said, "Yeah, yeah. Just make sure I'm looking beyond fresh for my pretty, black doll."

"Whatever, nigga."

By the time he finished, a brother looked clean as hell. He killed my damn edges. Once he left, I stared at myself in the mirror, making sure there was nothing else I needed to do to be perfect for her. I'd even gotten a manicure. Chinara deserved the best of me in every aspect. Since I'd already given it to her raw, I didn't really have a gift, but up until this point, besides paying her bills, I hadn't really bought her anything. Her ring didn't count as a gift. But Saturday, I planned to take her shopping in Houston. I noticed that she didn't really have a lot of clothes or shoes and she deserved to be able to have so much to wear until it took her hours to decide.

After my shower, the phone rang. It was Chinara, probably wanting me to stay out of sight. "Hello?"

"Hi, baby. I'm outside."

"Okay. Do you want the master bedroom?"

"Please?"

"Okay. Let me get my stuff for tomorrow out of here. Give me a few minutes, then come on in."

"I miss you already."

I chuckled, but I knew she was serious. Whenever I got home from work in the evenings, we would be glued at the hip. We took showers together almost every day. I didn't mind because I loved being with her, too. "I miss you, too, Pretty Black."

I ended the call, then got my suit, beard oil, and other essentials for tomorrow and made my way to the room she slept in when she first got here. When I heard the backdoor close, it took everything in me not to leave this room to greet her. She'd insisted that I went out and had a bachelor party with my boys, but I wasn't feeling that. My entire adult life had been a bachelor party. Whenever I had free time, I found myself in a strip club, at a party, or in something hot and gushy. I was all partied out... fucking sick of it.

Any partying I did from now on would include my life-partner... or at least I hoped she would be. She still had the option to bounce once I got my inheritance and gave her what I promised her. I was pretty confident right now, but within the next six months, I could possibly get on her damn nerves. The knock at the door startled me and I got happy as hell. As I made my way to it, she said, "Don't open the door, Haji. Just come to it."

When I got to the door, I rested my forehead on it, because I could imagine that was what she was doing. Resting my palms on it, I said, "I'm here, Chinara."

"I know. I can feel you."

No more words were spoken for a few minutes, but it was like I could feel her, too. I was in love with this woman and I planned to tell her soon. I just hoped she would say it back.

 hinara

"I'M gonna leave so you can move around the house freely. Jarius is here to pick me up."

"Okay. Thank you, Haji."

When I heard the backdoor close, I began running around the house trying to figure out how I was gonna drive in my dress and stressing. Before I could stress too much, Haji called. "Hey, baby. You forgot something?"

"Yeah. To tell you that I got a car to pick you up. It should be there in two hours."

"What a relief. Thank you."

He chuckled, then said, "Calm down, Pretty Black. Take some deep breaths. You could drive your car and show up in blue jeans and a t-shirt for all I care."

It was my turn to chuckle. "I wouldn't dare. See you in a little while."

"A'ight."

I was beyond excited to be marrying Haji. Only two weeks ago, I thought he was crazy as hell, but I was thankful because of the predicament I was in. Our intentions were kind of messed up, but now... I was almost sure he loved me. I loved his ass, too. I was so attached to everything about Haji until when he left for work, I would move to his side of the bed just to inhale his scent. My understanding of this situation was cloudy as hell. How could I have fallen for a man this damn fast? He told me to free-fall, but that shit was nowhere near graceful. I fell without a parachute.

Going to the bathroom, I was excited about applying my makeup. I hadn't done it in a long time. Before I could get started, the doorbell rang. Frowning slightly, I made my way back downstairs. Someone was at the front door. No one ever went to the front door. I cautiously approached and looked out the side window. It was a man, two women, and a kid. When the man's eyes met mine, I quickly moved away from the window. He had to be Haji's brother. They looked alike. Hesitantly opening the door, the older woman standing there smiled. "Hi, Chinara!"

At that moment, I realized she was Haji's mother. He couldn't have known they were coming. "Hi! Wow! Haji didn't tell me to expect you! Come in!"

The four of them walked in with huge smiles on their faces, looking around the house. "Wow. You're even more beautiful in person! You can call me Afiong. I don't think I ever told you my name. This is Haji's oldest brother, Umaru, his wife, Taj, and their daughter, Imani."

I smiled big and shook their hands. Taj smiled big and asked, "What time do you have to be there?"

"A car is coming to pick me up in one hour and forty-five minutes."

"Oh! Let's help her get ready, Mama!" Taj said excitedly.

Excitement and joy filled my heart. I was already feeling a way about not having my mama and sister here but having someone here for me had melted my heart. "Yes! Please! Umaru, make yourself comfortable."

Taj hurried me up the stairs as we giggled like schoolgirls. Imani and Ms. Afiong followed us up. When we got to the room, Haji's mother said, "My son did extremely well for himself."

"He did. This house is amazing."

"I was talking about you. You have a beautiful spirit."

I lowered my head as I smiled. "Thank you. I did well for myself also."

"Okay, okay. Enough of that. Let's get this makeup done before we're late. I love doing makeup, and I would love to do yours if you're okay with that," Taj said.

"Sure," I said with a smile, hoping I wasn't making a mistake.

I knew nothing about Taj, but she had that big sister vibe going on. I'd always wanted a big sister. After getting comfortable and allowing her to work her magic, I watched Haji's mother have a fit over my dress. It was a mermaid-style dress, that accentuated my every curve. There was a single golden strap that would go across my chest, then across my back. The pattern of the dress was Kente cloth down the front and in the slits of the dress, but the predominant color was green. "Chinara, this dress is beautiful."

"Thank you."

I smiled as she and Imani talked about the dress and our upcoming nuptials. Haji was on my mind heavily and as if he knew that, he sent a text. *I think Chinara Abimbola has a nice ring to it. What do you think?*

I think it has an amazing ring to it. I can't wait to bring you honor while carrying it.

Because of the way I was brought up to believe in marriage, this ceremony today was practically normal. People in Nigeria didn't often marry for love. They married to procreate... providing to the society by having children. I never liked that tradition and I was grateful that my parents hadn't already picked someone for me to marry. It was how they got married. Love came later. When I got old enough to understand, I always knew that I wanted to know what it felt like to be in love. I wanted to marry someone I was in love with. "Okay. What do you think?"

Taj stepped away from me and my eyes widened. "Oh my God! I look gorgeous."

My eyes were starting to mist, and she said, "Oh no. You will not mess up this makeup."

We all laughed as I looked at the green and orange accents in my eyeshadow. I looked like an African queen and I knew Haji was going to love it. "Okay, let's help you get this dress on," Ms. Afiong said.

Thankfully, my hair was already done. I'd gotten it straightened yesterday and it was practically to my ass. Wrapping it last night was a real headache, but it was worth it. As she helped me step into my dress, she asked, "So, how long have you and Haji known one another?"

"Not very long, but he said when he first saw me a little over three months ago, he knew I was the one."

Things became awkward for a moment and I knew they would. Had I not loved Haji, I wouldn't have been honest about the amount of time. As I adjusted my breasts in the dress, I decided to say something. Clearly, Haji's father hadn't died when we first met. So he didn't talk to me simply because of that. "But I suppose amount of time isn't important when your feelings are as deep as mine and Haji's. He's the man I'd been longing for my whole life."

I refused to tell them I loved him before I told him. I wanted him to be the first to know how I felt. "I can clearly see that you love him. I was just ill-prepared for your response," Haji's mother said.

I smiled softly at her, then got my headpiece to wear. It was gold and small trinkets hung from it, one of them right between my eyebrows. After looking in the mirror, I turned to them and asked, "How much time do I have left?"

"Ten minutes," Taj responded.

I nodded at her, then took a selfie to send to my family. "Let me take a full-length picture of you," Taj offered.

"Thank you."

I handed my phone to her and she took the picture. "I guess we should head down and wait for the car," I said to the ladies.

They agreed as I turned lights off. I felt like royalty walking down the stairs in this dress. I couldn't wait to see Haji's reaction to not only the dress, but to his family being here as well.

———

WHEN WE GOT THERE, my nerves had kicked in. I was hot and on the verge of sweating as I stood outside, about to walk inside. Taj wanted to make sure I was still well put-together before walking through the doors. After explaining to her that we could do this on the inside, she laughed and said, "You're right. You're gonna be melting in a minute."

Once everyone exited the Rolls Royce Haji had rented, we walked inside. Could have sworn we were King Jaffe Joffer and Queen Aoleon the way people stopped and stared at us. I even noticed a few people taking pictures. Haji definitely made sure that I felt like a queen. After getting past security, the court we were going into was to the left. Standing outside of it, I looked at the clock in the middle of the lobby area to see I only had five minutes. Taj quickly pat my face with a sponge, then had me close my eyes so she could spray it with a setting spray.

I was at the point of trembling, scared to reveal my true feelings to Haji, but there was no other time that would be more perfect. Just the fact that we'd moved this date up was evidence to me that he loved me, too. We were supposed to wait a month and it had only been three weeks. Glancing back at his mother and niece in their African garb, I smiled. Taj had on hers, too. Umaru's suit had a Kente pattern on the lapels. So, it was obvious that we were dripping with our African heritage. "You ready, sister-in-law?"

I took a deep breath and exhaled, then said, "Absolutely."

Umaru opened the door and I slowly walked through. The

moment I walked around the wall and saw Haji standing there in a cream-colored suit with a print the same pattern as mine draped across his body, I nearly succumbed to the tears. He obviously felt the same way as he pressed his palms together, bringing them to his face. However, before I could get to him, he noticed his family behind me. The tears that left his eyes, let me know just how overwhelming this was for him. While he'd shown me his sensitive side, he never struck me as the type to cry.

When I got to him, he grabbed my hand as he went to his knee, bowing before me. He was gonna have me crying. I was fighting hard not to let them fall. Taj had my phone, taking pictures and I noticed Haji's friend, Jarius had a professional-looking camera, taking pictures as well. After kissing my hand Haji stood to his feet and stared in my eyes. Lifting my hand to his cheek, I wiped away the tears that had fallen from his eyes. "You're so beautiful, Queen."

"Thank you. You look amazing yourself," I said, then bowed my head.

I knew he wouldn't have too much to say about me following tradition in this moment, especially since he'd bowed in my presence. When I looked back up at him, he smiled at me, then slid his hand over the hair on my bare shoulder. The judge began preliminaries and I honestly didn't hear a word, other than the fact that he'd pronounced my last name right. My focus was on Haji the entire time. When Haji squeezed my hands, I realized I'd missed something important.

My eyebrows lifted slightly as the judge chuckled. "Chinara do you have any words you'd like to say to your groom?"

I nodded, then turned my attention back to Haji. Smiling, I said, "I surely thought you had lost your mind when you first called me Pretty Black Doll. My attitude was on ten. Then I realized, *What are tripping for? That's a compliment.*"

Everyone chuckled along with me. "Haji, you are like no man I've ever met. I couldn't have even dreamed of a man more perfect for me than you. Not saying that we won't disagree, but I feel like even our disagreements will be handled in love. Thank you for choosing me to be your queen... to be the woman that you want to spend the rest of your life with. I promise that I will do my best to elevate you when you're down... make you happy when you're sad... encourage you through your disappointments. I love you, Haji Abimbola."

The tears dropped from my eyes as Haji stared at me. The love he felt for me was evident and I could tell that he probably expected me to profess my love for him at this moment. Now that I had, I expected him to reciprocate it. I could clearly see it through his gaze. "Mr. Abimbola, you may express your words to your bride."

Bringing my hand to his lips, he kissed it and began, "From the moment I saw you leaving Hair World, I knew. My exact thoughts were, *This is the woman that will change my life forever.* That was before you even opened your mouth. Your beauty is an attention-getter for sure. You look like a pretty, black doll. Before knowing your given name, it was what I referred to you as. But the moment you frowned at me and you opened your mouth, shooting me down in Black woman fashion, I said, *Aww yeah. She the one!*"

I laughed as did everyone else. My cheeks had heated up tremendously. Although this marriage was rushed because of the circumstances, it felt so right, like the timing was perfect. "When I realized what you were going through at the time, I knew I had to step up and be the man you didn't think I was. I had to show you that I wasn't just a playa tryna holla at you. I was tryna build with you, Pretty Black. Every moment around you has made me weaker and weaker for you. I've never experienced these types of feelings for a woman until you. I promise to take care of you to the best of my abilities, making you happy, not feeling a moment of regret about sharing your life with me. I love you, Chinara, and I plan to show you just how much for the rest of my life."

The tears were dropping uncontrollably from my eyes. I couldn't believe we'd gotten to this moment so soon. To hear him say he loved me was the icing on the cake. Feeling it was one thing, but his acknowledgement of it took it to a new level. Taj walked up to us to pat my cheeks with Umaru's handkerchief. The judge smiled, then continued with the ceremony. We exchanged gorgeous wedding bands, and Jarius laid a broom at our feet. Before jumping it, the judge pronounced us husband and wife and before he could get the words out, saying Haji could salute his bride, Haji put his hands to my face and pulled me to him, kissing me with so much passion it was mind-blowing.

When we finally separated and I'd gathered my composure, we jumped the broom. His family then ran to him, sweeping him away from me in their embraces. I smiled, seeing how happy he was to see them there. Jarius came to me and congratulated me, along with Kline and a couple of other friends of his. Once he'd taken a couple of pictures, Haji joined me once again for some couple's photos. "I thought I would be the one to say it first," he said.

I smiled at him, bringing my hand to his face. "Well, surprise, surprise. However, you made me feel loved immediately. I hope that I made you feel the same."

"I wouldn't say I felt it immediately, but by day two at my house, I felt it."

I chuckled because I was trying to be tough at first. He lifted my head and kissed my lips. "I love you, Pretty Black Doll."

"I love you, too, Haji. I'm gonna have to come up with a nickname for you."

"Naw, that's alright. If it doesn't come natural, I don't want it. Besides, I love the way Haji rolls off these succulent lips."

"Okay. You starting already, but your family is here."

"And? I can assure you that they will be here at least a week. I have time for them. But I need to get at my wife ASAP. We already missed last night."

He pulled me closer to him, staring in my eyes. The love and lust between us were overwhelming and the heat was taking over. "A'ight, come on and take a picture with your fam, bruh," Jarius said.

Haji kissed my lips again and went to his family. After one picture, I joined them. He also took a few shots with his friends.

Once they were done, we left the courthouse. Jarius agreed to transport his family and Haji and I had the Rolls Royce to ourselves. The moment we were inside, Haji's lips collided with mine and I was almost sure he was gonna take me to ecstasy in this car. His hand palmed my breast, then slid to my neck, giving me a slight preview of what was to come. "I don't know if I'll be able to take my time, baby. My battery seems to be down to about twenty percent. That warning light done came on, telling me I need to connect to the source. I need a power charge."

"My body is yours to do with as you please, baby. I know that I'll be pleased either way."

"Girl... shit," he said as he grabbed at his dick.

I knew I was about to be in a world of trouble and everyone in the house was gonna know it.

17

Haji

CARRYING my wife over the threshold at my house garnered cheers from my family and friends. I didn't waste any time fooling around with nobody. Going straight to the stairs with her, everyone laughed and cheered loudly. Hopefully, they decided to go somewhere away from the house or go outside. If they didn't, somebody was gon' have to explain to my lil niece what sounds or screams she heard. "Haji! You don't want to be cordial first?" Chinara said as she laughed.

"Hell naw. Today is our day. They can wait."

I continued up the stairs and down the hallway to our bedroom. Once inside, I set her on her feet, then closed and locked the door. Grabbing my phone, I started a little playlist I made for this moment... this day. "Make Love" by Hamilton Park was the first track and I knew I probably wouldn't hear shit else after that. Walking over to her, I spun her around and unzipped her dress, allowing my fingers to graze her skin. She looked like royalty and I planned to treat her as such when I pleased her body.

Sliding my hands around her, I grabbed her breasts as she leaned back against me, bringing her hands to the back of my head. The sensuality of that had me wanting to fuck her up... like now. But I knew this was a moment we would never get back. I wanted this to be memorable. Moving her hair, I began kissing her neck softly, then inched up to her ear, pulling the lobe between my teeth. "Haji... damn," she whispered.

Pulling away from her, I carefully pulled her dress off, then draped it over the closet door. I did the same with my shirt, tuxedo jacket, and pants as I admired the gorgeous woman standing before me. Seeing her in only her head garb, thong, and heels was causing me to leak. Although we'd never really talked about having children, today would be the day she would surely get pregnant if she wasn't on the pill. When she entered that courtroom today, my soul surrendered to the hold she had over me. Her dress and the golden jewels wrapped around her head only accented her beauty. Not to mention the way her face was made up.

Walking back to her, I licked my lips, preparing to bring our bodies places they'd never seen. When I reached her, I kissed her lips and allowed my hands to travel slowly down her back until they reached their intended destination... that fat-ass peach. Squeezing it, I deepened my kiss, my tongue caressing her spirit. At least that was what it felt like. It seemed we kissed for a good five minutes or longer without separating. My heart was open from here to Africa for this woman. When I finally separated from her lips, I began a slow and sensuous trail to her most intimate parts.

Pulling that dark chocolate in my mouth, I sucked it, inciting a slow rhythm that had her grasping my head. Slowly backing her to the bed, I began pulling at her thong, pulling it to her thighs. The crotch was wet with her juices and I was beyond ready to taste her. As she stepped out of them, I pulled them to my face, sniffing them, craving her essence to fill my mouth. She sat on the bed, then scooted back, widening her legs for me. "Fuck, baby. You ready for me?"

I slid my drawers off as she stared at me. "I'm beyond ready for you, King."

"King, huh?"

My shit bounced on my leg when she called me that. Her submission to me was overwhelming and something I never thought I wanted, but it was sexy as hell. "Yes. King. You don't wanna be that?"

"Oh, I am that. But it takes me to another place when you call me that."

"Well, don't leave me behind. Come and take me with you, baby."

That shit she was talking was gon' have me cumming quick as hell. Making my way to her, she quickly shifted her position, going to her knees in the bed and pulling my leaking dick into her mouth. "Mmmm," she moaned, causing my body to shiver.

I reached over and popped her ass as she arched her back, then gave it a squeeze. "Fuck!" I yelled as she applied the suction I liked.

Dropping my head back for a moment, I enjoyed the extra saliva she was coating me with. Looking down at her, my eyes met hers as she deep throated me. The back of her throat was paradise and watching her gag was like eating the forbidden fruit. I loved when she shook her head while it was deep in there. The head of my dick bouncing off the walls of her throat always took me to the point of no return. As she stroked the base of my dick, I could feel my nut rising to greet her.

I began slow fucking her mouth as I held her face in my hands. She began humming and I knew my kids were about to have a joyous time sliding down her throat. "Chinara... damn. I'm about to fill your throat with joy, baby."

She stared up at me like she was daring me to, and it didn't take long after that before I was growling out my release. Once I slid my dick from her lips, I flipped her over, and immediately brought my face to her precious jewel, getting a sample, before going back to her inner thighs. I loved her long ass legs, but I had to get a taste first. Her shit was gushy already and the way my taste buds were set up, I couldn't prolong having her flavor on my tongue. As I licked, sucked and nibbled her inner thighs, she squirmed in excitement, whispering loudly, "Fuck!"

I really loved when she started speaking her native tongue. That shit turned me on so much. Making my way back to her glistening pussy, I wanted to swallow that shit whole. Whispering against it, I said, "You're officially mine to fuck up."

Her pussy responded to me by excreting even more flavor for me to indulge in, so I got to it. I didn't want a drop more leaking to the bed. I needed all of that on my tongue. The moment my lips reached hers, she exhaled as if she'd been holding her breath. Her hands slid to the back of my head and she pushed me in further. Baby girl wasn't feeling the slow burn, either. She needed me to handle shit expeditiously. That was good to know. I slurped all her shit up and swirled my tongue around her clit before sucking it between my lips.

The screams emitting from her had my dick on swole, and I couldn't help but to stop and give him a taste. I quickly went to my knees and pushed inside of her as a chill went down my spine. "Fuck!"

"I love you, Haji. Shit!"

"I love you, too. Chinara."

I began stroking her as she scratched my back and wrapped her legs around my waist. After a few strokes, I pulled out and went back to eating her fruit. I digested quite a bit before I went back to her clit. Tongue kissing her shit, I sucked it hard and she shot that shit all over me. "Oh shit!" I said.

I knew she was just where I wanted her to be... engrossed in what I was doing to her and how she was feeling. She screamed as I pushed my dick back inside of her, taking advantage of the shit that was coming out of her like she'd sprung a leak. My mouth immediately went to her hard nipple and sucked it like it was giving me life. Her nails dug into my flesh on my shoulders as I growled and dug deeper inside of her. Hungrily kissing her lips, I gave her my tongue to share her excellence with her.

She used her hands to push me away and when I went to my back, my dick bounced around like, *what the fuck?* Not wasting time, she went to her knees and swallowed my shit. I felt like a bitch in here because I could barely handle it. My dick was so sensitive, she was gon' make me bust in her mouth again. Releasing me, Chinara climbed on top of me and slowly slid down my dick, her eyes rolling to the back of her head. She sat still for a moment, so I asked, "What'chu gon' do wit' it, Pretty Black?"

Her eyes opened and her hips rolled on me, stroking my dick to perfection from base to tip. Biting my bottom lip, I enjoyed the ride. Suddenly, she flattened her feet on the bed and began a slow bounce on my shit. Her balance was impeccable, and her pussy muscles squeezed the fuck outta my dick. I didn't know why she'd been holding out on me, but I was grateful she'd let loose on me now. Maybe she was saving her skills for marriage since she wasn't a virgin. Her pace got a little faster and I held onto her hips as I lifted my head to see what I was feeling.

Her juices were all over me and I was on the verge of nutting. I knew I would have to change this shit up before I did. My toes were curling as she handled me like a pro. When I felt myself getting too far, I slung her to the bed. Getting to my knees, I flipped her over and pulled her ass to me. When I saw the juices on her asshole, I lost focus. My tongue went right to it. I had never eaten out a female's ass, but Chinara could get it all. It seemed she liked that shit, too. Going back to my knees, I rubbed my dick over her asshole, and he twitched in excitement. *Naw, nigga. She ain't ready for that kind of activity.*

Sliding downward an inch, I pushed inside of her warmth. I straddled her legs and did some pushups on that pussy while she screamed from the thrusts. But when I went back to my knees and began rolling into her, I knew my dick had to be fucking up her ovaries. That was how deep it felt like I was. My growls and her screams had to be embarrassing the fuck out of everybody downstairs, but neither of us cared. The only thing that was on my mind was pleasing my wife and I was sure her mind was on pleasing her husband. I gently bit her shoulder and she screamed. "Damn, I love you, girl," I said as my hand gently gripped her neck.

Her whimpers only got me closer. "I love you, too, Haji!" she screamed as she came on my dick.

Felt like I'd just dipped my dick in Niagara Falls. Chinara was fucking me up with how sexual she was. "You love me? How come you was holding out on me? Huh?" I asked as plunged her pussy.

"You needed a gift from me for making me your wife. I knew you would love this gift... oh, fuck!" She was trying to explain while I was still beating her pussy like it stole something. "No more holding out on you, baby. You get every nasty drop of me. I hope you can handle it."

She arched her back, pushing her ass into me, giving me greater access to fuck her up. "Oh, you tryna tell me you a nasty-ass freak? I should've brought yo' ass to my hidden room and let you dance on that pole for daddy."

My dick felt like it was about to explode as my wife panted and screamed in response to my words in her ear and my dick in her pussy. "We got plenty of time for that and I can't wait to experience all that nasty shit with you. I'm about to cum, baby."

After a few more strokes into her pool of affection, I bust hard as hell, knowing that I'd definitely hit the fucking jackpot in choosing Chinara for my wife. I was grateful that she was with it, too.

MY FAMILY SURPRISING me meant the world to me. They'd never been to the United States to see me, so I never expected them to show up. When I noticed my mama and Umaru, I almost lost it. Crying in front of people wasn't something that I did. Hell, I barely cried when I was alone. So, for me to cry in front of everyone at the sight of them was a big deal.

After Chinara and I had a shower and stripped the bed, cleaning the mattress, we went downstairs to find everyone outside. The minute we walked out there my mama blushed. Yeah, they'd gotten an earful. "If yo' mama wasn't here, I'd tell you what I really thought of that sh... y'all just pulled," Jarius said with a frown on his face.

"Shut up."

I shook Umaru's hand and he stood and hugged me again. "So, Kevin still couldn't just let stuff go, huh?"

He shook his head. "I could tell he wanted to come when we all talked about it, but his pride wouldn't let him buy those tickets. I just don't know what's up with him and why he's so adamant about being against you in every-damn-thing. It's stupid to me."

I shrugged my shoulders. "His loss. My life gon' go on with this beautiful queen by my side."

"She is definitely that. I'm happy for you."

"Haji! I went home and cooked some rabbit after the ceremony since I knew your lady enjoyed it last time," Kline said as he walked on the patio with a huge pot.

Chinara squealed as she hopped up and down. Shaking my head slowly, I said, "Thanks, man. That's what's up. Let me cook some rice."

"I already cooked rice, Haji, along with a beef stew. Me and Imani had Jarius take us to the store when you two got unbearable."

She blushed again and I laughed. "Thanks, Ma. I appreciate that." I looked around and said, "Well y'all come on back inside."

Chinara walked ahead of me, but I gently grabbed her ponytail that she'd put her hair in, halting her progress. Looking at her in those leggings and t-shirt always had me wanting to feel her up. Shit, it didn't matter what she wore. I would still want to let my hands roam her gorgeous curves. She turned to me with a smile on her face, then she dropped her head for a moment. Now understanding why she always did that, it didn't bother me as much. I began doing the same to her because I honored her as well. She was my queen, and in my house, she had just as much authority as I did.

I pulled her close to me and kissed her lips, then rubbed my thumb over her bottom one as she tilted her head back. "You are so amazing to me. So, beautiful and so perfect for me."

"You are the same to me also, my love," she said as she ran her fingers through my beard.

"Man, if y'all don't come on so we can eat. Y'all had almost three hours to get that out earlier. Surely, y'all can make it an hour or two without tryna hop each other's bones," Jarius said.

I knew that was the clean version of what he really wanted to say. We chuckled and made our way inside as Taj and Mama fixed plates. "Kline, this is rabbit?" Taj asked.

"Yes, ma'am. Once you taste it, you'll be in heaven."

"Taj, he's so right about that. I looove it," Chinara said as I slid my arms around her waist.

"Man, let the woman breathe. She can't get a foot away from you before you trying to subdue her."

"Jarius, you 'bout to be up outta here in a minute."

I laughed and let Chinara free from my grasp, but only until we were done eating. They could all kiss my ass. As long as my baby didn't have a problem with it, then that was exactly where I was gonna be... all up under her.

hinara

WATCHING Haji interact with his family was refreshing and I couldn't wait until I could see my family. He was having an amazing time with his brother. I wondered if he would ever repair the relationship with his other brother, Kevin. The whole thing just seemed so petty to me. But whatever. Who was I to get involved? I didn't know his brother like that. It could run a lot deeper than it seemed from the outside looking in. As I sat talking to Taj and Imani, Haji winked at me. I felt my face heat up as I blew a kiss at him. I felt like I was back in high school, being in love for the first time. "Y'all are too cute."

"Thank you. How long have you and Umaru been married?"

"Ten years in a couple of months. And he's been amazing. Hopefully, Haji takes after him as a husband."

"He's good to me and has been since before he asked me to marry him." I had to get off that subject. Taj had made me extremely comfortable around her and I didn't want to slip and say something I shouldn't. "What's up with Kevin?"

"Girl, I don't know. As long as I've been around the family, they never got along, but I did notice that Kevin started most of the drama. I think he's jealous of Haji in some way. I only remember one time that Haji threw shit in his face. He'd come home from college to visit and he told Kevin that if he could get off his mama's tit long enough, he could become a man."

She laughed and I chuckled because it sounded like something Haji would say. "It wasn't funny then, because they started fighting after he said that, but it's so funny now. Papa Ense was pissed. He was always harder on Haji, though, I never understood why. Haji is the youngest, but it seemed as if Kevin was the one who was spoiled."

Hmm. That was weird. Maybe it was the middle child thing. Not only was he the middle child, but he was small in stature according to his pictures on Instagram. Umaru was at least six inches taller than him in one of the pictures. Haji was the same height as Umaru. Also, Haji and Umaru looked alike. Kevin didn't look that much like them to me. They had similar features but nothing that would have someone thinking they were brothers. "Well, I hope they can one day get it together."

"That would be totally up to Kevin. Haji has tried to be cordial, but Kevin just won't grow up. He's thirty-four or thirty-five and still can't act like a grown man at times. He and Umaru have gotten into it, but mostly about how Kevin treats Haji."

She shook her head. "Mommy, can I have more to eat?"

"I thought you wanted to swim? You can't swim if you eat more."

"Well, maybe we can swim tomorrow."

I chuckled. That rabbit was off the grid. It was smothered this time and I think I loved it more this way than boiled in the seafood seasoning. It had a thick gravy and tasted amazing with rice. "Imani, I think I'm gonna join you for seconds. It was so good."

She giggled as we went to the kitchen for seconds. As I fixed her plate, Haji appeared behind me. He kissed my neck and said, "Today has been perfect. Tomorrow I had planned to take you to Houston to go shopping, but since my family is here, we'll have to postpone that. I also booked our tickets for Lagos. We'll be leaving in two weeks."

After giving Imani her plate, I turned to him and hugged him tightly. I kissed his lips and said, "Thank you so much. I really wish they could have been here."

"I'm sorry. I didn't even think to ask."

"They don't have passports, so they wouldn't have been able to come anyway."

"Well, we are going to see what we can do for them. I know you love your family. Do you think they would be open to coming to the US? How old is your sister?"

The tears left my eyes. The deal was for me to become successful so I could help them. That hadn't happened and I was stuck here because I didn't have enough money to go home. Since Haji was an American citizen, I was too now. "I think they would love it here. My sister is twenty-five. She's dedicated her life to taking care of my parents. I send money when I can, but I was supposed to be successful by now where I could help them more."

"Don't cry, baby. We'll talk about this later. Okay?"

"Okay."

"Fix your rabbit and enjoy yourself. You and Taj seem to be getting along."

"We are. God, I love you," I said, then kissed his lips.

He slapped my ass, then winked at me. "I love you more."

When he walked away, I took a deep breath. Bringing my parents and sister here would mean the world to me. They were living in poverty in Lagos, barely surviving. I couldn't wait to talk to Haji more about it tonight and talk to them tomorrow. After fixing my food, I went to the table and sat next to Ms. Afiong. Before I could start eating, she grabbed my hand. "I just wanted to say that you are most definitely the one for him. The happiness on his face and the glow on his skin... it's something I've never seen. I also apologize for what Kevin did. Taj told me about it. I must admit, I had my doubts because this seemed to happen so quickly, but there's no doubt in my mind now."

I smiled at her. Being that I was already emotional, the tears slid down my cheeks. She put her hands to my face and said, "I can see how much you love him as well. The way you respect him and love him is beautiful to watch. I've been watching you two since you came downstairs. The winks and kisses being blown across the room is heartwarming. I'm sorry. I interrupted your meal. Eat up. We have so much to talk about."

I smiled and blessed my food. Hopefully, the 'so much' we had to talk about would be just getting to know one another.

"Daraja!"

"Hey, sis! We've been waiting to hear from you! How are you?"

"I'm good. I have Haji sitting next to me. Say hello."

She cleared her throat and took a deep breath, then said, "Hello, Haji. So nice to make your acquaintance."

I rolled my eyes at how she'd changed her voice. He chuckled slightly, then said, "Hello, Daraja."

"How are y'all, sis?"

"We're okay. Since you sent that money, we were able to get the things we needed. Thank you, Nara."

"You don't have to thank me. Where's Mama and Papa?"

"They are in the front room. I'm heading in there."

I sat in Haji's arms excited as hell with what I was about to say to them. We'd talked last night, and he'd surprised me by some of the things he said. "Chi Chi!" Papa yelled. "How are you?"

"I'm so good, Papa. How are you?"

"Good, since I know that you are good."

"Hi, Nara!"

"Hey, Mama. How are you feeling?" I asked, noticing that her voice sounded somewhat weak.

"I'm hanging in there. I feel dizzy and weak a lot, but the doctors are having a hard time treating me because I can't pay them. They patch me up with some medicine for a temporary fix and send me on my way."

Closing my eyes, I took a deep breath. She was getting worse. Diabetes was destroying her body. The tear fell from my eye and Haji wiped it, then softly kissed my cheek. "That's no good, Mama. Umm, Haji is on the phone."

"Hello, Mr. and Mrs. Nwachuku."

"Hello," they both said in unison.

My parents were extremely guarded when it came to meeting new people. So, they were completely silent after that. I chuckled and said, "Haji bought us plane tickets. We'll be seeing you guys in two weeks. Oh, and umm... we got married yesterday."

I could hear Daraja screaming in excitement in the background and I could imagine that she was running and jumping all over the house. Mama was laughing and I assumed it was at Daraja's theatrics. "Haji, thank you. I haven't seen my Chi Chi in ten years. This means more than you could ever know."

"It's my pleasure, Mr. Nwachuku."

"Papa, there's more."

Everyone was quiet, waiting for what I would say. "While we are there, we will apply for passports and Visas. I... we would like for y'all to move here with us. Mama will get better care and Daraja will be able to live her life and pursue her dreams. Plus, I'll get to see you guys all the time."

There was complete quietness. Then Daraja asked, "Where would we live?"

"Haji has a five-bedroom home. Besides his room, two of the other bedrooms have their own bathrooms. You would have privacy. And he has a huge kitchen."

"We... Chinara. *We* have enough room in *our* home to accommodate all of you."

I leaned over to him and softly kissed his lips. This man was so good to me. As we waited for their response, there was a knock at our bedroom door. Haji went to answer it and I saw his mother standing there. After a brief exchange, he came back to me. Kissing my shoulder, he slid the covers from over me and began caressing his favorite spots. I almost moaned. I pushed his hand away as he smirked. Finally, my mama said, "Haji, can we think about it and give you an answer by the time the two of you come to visit?"

"Sure. Take as much time as you need. I understand that it's a lot to uproot yourself from all you've ever known."

I knew that if the decision had been up to Daraja, she'd be at the airport trying to hop a flight without a ticket. "Mama, please think about it. I want you to be around a lot longer and I can tell by your voice that you aren't feeling well. I love all of you and just want what's best. But if you choose to stay there in Lagos, I won't be angry. I'll do whatever I can to help you financially."

"We love you, too. And we will seriously think about it," Papa said.

I could hear movement like someone was walking, then a door close. "Listen, sis. I'm gon' talk them into it. If it were up to me, I'd have you transfer those flights to us, and we'd be there as soon as those passports came in. I'm tired, Chinara. I just want to live."

"I know, sis. Work on them. I love you."

"I love you more."

I ended the call and allowed the tears to fall from my eyes. "Don't cry, Pretty Black. Whatever they decide, we'll have to be okay with it. Okay?"

"Yeah."

He pulled me back to the bed as I smelled food. I assumed his mother had come to the door to say she would be cooking breakfast. My stomach growled loudly, and he frowned. "Damn, girl. You hungry? Shit."

I playfully slapped his arm. "I'm starving. After last night and this morning, I would like to say I worked up an appetite."

He chuckled and pulled me in his arms and said, "Hell yeah. My dick was thoroughly satisfied, but his ass greedy. He winking at'chu now."

I slowly shook my head, then disappeared under the covers and pulled his drawers down over his erection. He'd been inside of me so much the last few hours, my scent had taken over him. Slowly sliding my mouth over it, I lubed him up really good, then began pleasing my man how he liked it. Each time I gave him head, I tried to get better. His groans propelled me forward and let me know that I was doing something right. Surprisingly, I found out last night that he liked to feel my teeth occasionally... not an overwhelming amount, just enough to lightly glide along his length, reminding him that he was in my mouth.

Throwing the covers off me, Haji grabbed ahold of my hair and said, "Damn, baby. You handling a nigga like this early this morning? Fuck!"

I moaned on him, feeling the head of his dick pulsate. Teasing it, I only sucked the head, making him grip my hair tighter as he tried to remain quiet. I loved hearing him express himself during sex. Quickly pulling me off his dick, he flipped me over and immediately slid inside of me. Lying on my side, I closed my eyes and moaned. Haji lifted my leg, then said in a low voice near my ear, "This love shit between us is untamable. I feel like I'll fuck you anywhere. I love you, Pretty Black."

"I love you, too," I panted.

Putting my leg over his shoulder, he leaned over to tease my nipple with his tongue as his dick, nearly paralyzed me into submission. I hadn't had dick until I met his. That bullshit before this had to be just penis or cock. It had to have a certain skill and size to be considered a dick. And this shit Haji was putting on me was *all* dick. "O kan lara daraaa... mu funmi."

I didn't even know if he knew what I'd said at first, but it was apparent when he started stroking me harder and deeper. Telling him, *it felt so good* and to *give it to me* in Yoruba brought out the African beast in him. My moans had gotten louder, and my nails were digging into whatever part of him I could grasp. After biting my earlobe, he said, "Ahhh fuck! I hope you on the pill. I'm 'bout to put triplets in yo' shit."

I smiled slightly. I didn't take birth control pills, so whatever happened was just gonna happen. Before I could respond, I came... hard. "Hajiiiii! Fuck!!"

He quickly covered my mouth, because my screams of passion could have been heard down the street. That orgasm snuck up on me and wiped me out. My muffled sounds and my wide eyes must have done something to him because, shortly after, I had to cover his mouth. He pounded into me hard and gripped my hips tightly as he released his seed. If I wasn't so dark-complexioned, I would surely see bruises where his fingers had dug into my flesh. Collapsing beside me, he grabbed my hand and kissed it. "I'll have all of the babies you want, King."

He turned to me and said, "You saying that now."

After chuckling, he turned to me and kissed my forehead, then my nose, and finally my lips. "I'm good with two, but if you want more, we can make that happen."

"My womb is open to you. And I can't wait to carry your legacy, Haji Okiro Abimbola."

aji

THE NINETEEN-HOUR FLIGHT had wiped us out. When we got to the hotel in Lagos, we took a nap before calling her family. I supposed had I let her sleep the night before we left, we would have been more rested, but I couldn't get enough of her. Sleep was broken a lot on the flight, because every time the plane jerked, Chinara woke up, panicking. Since she hadn't flown in years, she'd forgotten that sometimes the slight turbulence only meant we could be flying through clouds. Regardless of that fact, it was still turbulence and could have a bad result. Because she was nervous, it made me nervous.

My family had stayed for a week after the wedding and Chinara, Mama, and Taj were like the three musketeers with their broke best friend, Imani. They'd spent time getting their hair done, going to the spa and shopping. Surprisingly, Mama funded their activities. She obviously wasn't as tight with money as my dad had been. That nigga was tight as hell, like we were a step below the poverty level. Umaru and I seemed to get even closer during the time they were here. We spent more time together than we had in years and he really enjoyed his first trip to America.

When I stirred awake from my nap, Chinara was staring at me with a huge smile on her face. We'd gotten a room at the Radisson Blu Anchorage Hotel and the bed was extremely comfortable. I'd slept like a baby. We'd gotten a suite with a lagoon view, that way her family could spend time with us here during the day. Their home didn't have air conditioner and it was hot as hell outside. I didn't know how in the hell they were surviving in this heat. Gently sliding my hand over her cheek, I said, "Have you called them?"

"No. I was waiting for you to wake up."

"How long did I sleep?"

"I slept an hour and you slept another hour after me."

"Make the call, Pretty Black."

I kissed her forehead, then she hopped up from the bed. When she called, she started screaming and dancing, telling her sister that we were here and for them to get dressed. I chuckled as I watched her. She was so excited, and I hated that she had to go so long without seeing her family. They seemed extremely close. We'd rented an SUV because her family didn't own a car. That way we could transport them back and forth. We would be here for a little over a week and depending on how her mom felt would determine what all we did.

I hadn't been here in a long time and it was just as hot as I remembered it being. So, hopefully, most of our activities wouldn't be outdoors. When Chinara ended the call, she hopped in the bed and fell on top of me as I laughed. She was so happy, and I was happy that I could help put that joy in her heart. "So, are we going to get them, or will you send a car for them?"

"We're gonna go get them. What time is it?"

"Good. I wanted to see what condition the house was in. And it's noon."

"Okay. Well, let's get going. We have reservations at five and we have to prepare before that."

"Reservations where? At a restaurant? Does my family know?"

"Slow down, baby. Everything is handled."

I kissed her forehead and got up from the bed, then pulled her up as well. Pulling her close, I said, "I'm so happy that you're happy. I can't wait to see your face later."

She frowned slightly and it caused me to chuckle. She had no idea what she was in store for. "Haji, what do you have planned?"

"Just know that you will love it. Okay?"

"Okay," she said hesitantly.

We exited the hotel and she directed me to her parents' home. When we got there, I understood their reasons for getting her to America. Their home was in horrible condition. The joy on Chinara's face had turned into sadness as she looked at it. If a strong wind came through, it looked like it would fall to the ground. "I can't believe none of them ever told me just how bad the house was."

"Things are about to change, baby. Come on."

We got out of the car and headed to the door. Before we could knock, the young lady I took for her sister flung the door open and practically jumped on her. She looked a lot like Chinara but wasn't as dark-complexioned. She was still chocolate, but she lacked that rich-ness my baby had. After they screamed for what felt like eternity in this heat, Daraja finally looked over at me, lowered her head, and said, "Hello, Haji."

I pulled her into a hug. "Girl, if you don't quit playing."

She laughed loudly, then invited us in. Mr. Nwachucku was standing there with a huge smile on his face. Chinara ran to him and hugged him tightly as a woman came from the back, using a cane. The tears fell from Chinara's eyes as she looked at her mother. I could tell that she'd been in bad health for a while. Her body may not be able to take such a long flight. Mr. Nwachuku came to me and shook my hand, then suddenly pulled me into an embrace. That caught me off-guard. I'd never hugged my dad as an adult. The last time I remembered hugging him was after my high school graduation. "Nice to meet you, Mr. Abimbola."

I smiled. "Nice to meet you also, Mr. Nwachuku."

"I appreciate you immensely. Thank you for everything you have done to help our family. I promise, you won't know we are even there," he said right before Daraja started screaming. "Well, you won't know me and Bukola are there."

I laughed and said, "Well, Chinara has no clue about you all joining us or what festivities are going on today."

He smiled, then said, "I suppose we should get going then."

When I turned to get Chinara, Mrs. Nwachuku was standing there. She pulled me in her arms and hugged me tightly as her cane fell to the floor. "You are an amazing man, and I'm glad to have you as a son."

I kissed her cheek and said, "I'm grateful to have you as a second mother. Let's get our day started."

She smiled brightly as I escorted her out of the house to the SUV. It was easier to seat her in the front seat. I was sure Chinara didn't mind. She and Daraja hadn't stopped talking yet. Once we were all in, Chinara asked, "Haji, where are we going?"

Everyone kind of chuckled and as she looked around, she realized everyone knew about today's festivities but her. "Oh, this is messed up. All of you are keeping secrets from me."

She sat back and pouted. She would perk up soon enough. When we got to the venue, she looked around and saw flowers being carried in. Her facial expression read complete confusion. As we all got out of the vehicle, I went to her and pulled her in my arms. "Haji—"

I put my finger over her beautiful lips. "I need to explain something to you. Come over here for a second."

Looking back at her parents as they smiled, she stepped to the side with me. The stylists were arriving and carting all their materials inside. "The first time I asked you to marry me, it wasn't out of love.

Although I fell in love with you quickly and before the wedding happened, my intentions weren't based on love. This time, I wanna give you what you deserve. You deserve a traditional Nigerian wedding and a ceremony which will happen three days from now. I love you so much, baby, and I can't wait to see just how beautiful you will be. So, will you marry me, again?"

The tears were building in her eyes as she hugged me tightly. "This wasn't necessary, Haji. But since you did this, it's a testament to how much you love me."

"Okay, now go get ready," I responded, rushing her.

I slapped her ass as Daraja whisked her away. Her mother followed behind them looking extremely happy. Just as I was about to approach Mr. Nwachuku, I heard, "Haji!"

I turned to see Umaru, Mama, Taj, and Imani approaching us. After greeting me, Taj, Imani, and Mama went to join the women. As I shook Umaru's hand, I noticed Kevin, his wife, Bisa, and their two children, Fayola and Afolabi. My wall went up around my heart as Umaru stepped aside and allowed them to enter my space. He stretched his hand out to me and said, "Congratulations, brother."

I hesitantly shook his hand, waiting for the fuckery. When he released my hand, I hugged Bisa and their kids, then told Bisa and Fayola that they could join the women. I was sure the stylists had brought enough clothing and accessories for them as well. I introduced my brothers to Mr. Nwachuku and we all headed to our area to get ready. I didn't know what to make of Kevin being here, but he was extremely quiet. That was unusual as well, because he always had his mouth open, spitting venom and bullshit.

As we were walking inside the room, Kevin grabbed my arm and asked, "Can I talk to you? Privately?"

"Is it okay if Umaru comes to mediate?"

He chuckled slightly, but nodded and said, "Yeah."

I turned to Mr. Nwachuku and said, "Let the stylist get you set up. I'll be right back."

He nodded with a smile as Kevin instructed his son to stay with Mr. Nwachuku. When we walked into another room, I sat in a chair as did Kevin and Umaru. I was curious as hell about what he could possibly have to say. Me and the nigga hadn't talked to one another without arguing in years. He kind of fidgeted with his collar, then cleared his throat. "Umaru knows this, because obviously, he was born before me, but for some reason, Mom and Dad didn't want you to know. But I think had he told you, things might have been easier between us... less animosity. I was adopted. They adopted me about a year before Mama got pregnant with you. The doctors had told her that she wouldn't get pregnant again because she'd had such a hard time with Umaru."

I frowned immediately. So, Kevin's punk ass wasn't blood and he got treated better than me? I stood from my seat, fury consuming me. "Haji, I was jealous when you came along. At least that's what I was told. But as I got older, it got worse. When we were kids, I found out I was adopted by my biological father. My biological mother was Dad's sister. She'd left me on the doorstep when she moved. But she ended up getting killed not even two days later. They chose to raise me as their son. Mama probably coddled me too much and Daddy didn't make me really work for what I wanted. I think it was because they felt sorry for me."

Umaru had stood with me and put his hand on my shoulder, trying to calm me down. I sat back in my seat as Kevin continued. "Once I found out, I was jealous of you and felt like they would eventually forget about me because they had you. So, throughout life, I've always tried to be one up on you. The truth is, we don't have the same genetic makeup. You're smart as hell and headstrong just like Dad. I was always trying to prove myself and you didn't give a fuck. You were and still are strong enough to stand on your own, no matter who's with you or who isn't. I was afraid of failing, so I didn't want to take chances and go against Dad. I needed him and, in my mind, I felt like I needed him more than you. I'm so sorry for the way I've treated you over the years... our entire lives. Jealousy is a powerful emotion that can consume you and I allowed it to do just that."

He dropped his face in his hands for a moment and swiped them down it. Looking back at me as I tried to process everything he said, he continued. "I beg you for forgiveness and permission to be in your life as your brother."

I took a deep breath and exhaled. So, he was coddled because his parents were fuckups. What did that shit have to do with him? "I guess I'm a little lost. I don't understand what the point of being easy on you was. You didn't know at first. Had they treated you like they did me, no one would have noticed a difference."

"I was addicted to drugs as a baby. Back then, the only advice the doctor had was to gradually ween me off. They said the withdrawals could have killed me. So, I guess they were scared to lose me. Then after my biological dad showed up, they thought I was going to want to go live with him. He'd come to talk to them about taking me from them. I look just like his ass. Before he could make good on his threat, he died of an overdose. I was ten years old."

"We got into a huge fight when I was eight. I remember Dad beat the shit out of me because I broke your arm."

"The fight happened two days after I met him."

"Kevin, we're grown men. Why did this behavior continue? Regardless of blood, we're brothers. We're supposed to love and be there for one another."

"The behavior became a part of who I was. When you went to America, man... I developed a whole new level of hatred for you that I'm just finally trying to come out of. It took everybody, including my wife, alienating me to make me see the error of my ways... to understand the brotherhood I'd been missing out on. Now that I see it, I'm ashamed. I'm embarrassed at just how childish this is. I've pushed you over the years and I'm just grateful you never got the nerve to back up your words."

"What words?"

"That you'd kill me."

He smirked and I ended up grinning as well. Standing from my seat, I stretched out my hand to him. When he took it, I pulled him to his feet and embraced my brother for the first time in years. He patted my back as we hugged, and I did the same. "Let's just start fresh. Now come on so we can get ready for this Nigerian celebration."

hinara

HAJI HAD TOTALLY SURPRISED ME, and I couldn't stop the tears from accumulating in my eye ducts. The makeup artist was getting frustrated with me although she'd said she understood. This man had planned two entire weddings in my hometown of Lagos. I didn't know how he'd done it or where he'd found the time, but I was beyond emotional about all of it. The authentic ivory accessories that they placed on my head and hung around my neck was more than I could have ever imagined. We were all dressed in very stylish dresses made of Kente cloth. To say I was a loner, I had three women that would be standing with me along with two beautiful, little dolls.

I was beyond shocked when Kevin's wife and daughter had joined us. I didn't know who she was, but when Taj introduced her to me, I was stunned that they were here. I was shocked to see Ms. Afiong and Taj as well, especially since they'd come to the ceremony in Texas. But when I realized that Kevin was here with his family, I immediately thought about Haji and how things were going. I hadn't heard any commotion, and no one had come to get his wife, Bisa, or their daughter. So, I had to assume that everything was okay.

As the wedding planner led us and we approached the banquet hall of the venue, I could hear the tribal music and it sounded as if there were a lot of people in attendance. Turning to Daraja, I asked, "You helped him, didn't you?"

"Just with the guests and referrals on who to hire and the invitations and the food. But that's it."

I laughed loudly. She was his eyes and legs. "Sounds like you did all the leg work. Thank you, Daraja."

Shortly after, the planner alerted us that it was time to enter. I didn't know what the hell I was supposed to be doing, but thankfully, she talked us all through it. When I walked in and saw my man's chest partially out, I heated up. He was wearing a Kente cloth draped over one shoulder and one shoulder was out along with part of his chest. They allowed me to stand motionless for a moment, as the guests took me in and people approached me, wrapping me in silk and satin. There were people here that I went to high school with and that I'd worked with at old jobs as a teenager.

The decorations were gorgeous. It looked like I'd entered a tropical rainforest. The greenery and flowers covered the venue and I was in awe with just how beautiful it was. The scent of the food almost took me out, though. It had been a minute since I'd had goat. My stomach rumbled a little from the smell of the food, but my nerves were also on edge with at least two hundred people's eyes on me, analyzing every detail about me.

I was finally escorted to a chair that looked like it was on a thrown by two shirtless, male ushers like I was a queen. Once I sat, a group of people came out to dance to the tribal music as my husband bowed before my parents. When he stood, he approached me and bowed before me with a ring, like he was begging my hand in marriage. I already had two rings and by the time we were done here in Nigeria, I'd have more than I knew what to do with.

This wedding had all the makings of a traditional Nigerian wedding all the way down to him offering my parents gifts. I was beyond excited about everything and I knew my makeup had to be all messed up with as many tears that had dropped. As we relaxed into the wedding, the music changed. When the DJ spun "Next to Your Love" by Rotimi, the party started. Since Rotimi's parents were Nigerian, they damn near idolized him here.

As we danced, he held me by my hips, slightly grinding into me. Feeling him breathing on my neck had probably caused all the hairs back there to stand on end. "You know your sexy ass is mine tonight."

I turned to face him, resting my hands on his shoulders. "I'm yours whenever you want me. Didn't you say anytime, anyplace?"

"Girl, what'chu tryna say? You wanna fuck me at our wedding?"

"I'm saying... whenever you want me, I'm yours."

He swiftly pulled my hand from his shoulder and led me out the back door where he'd moved the SUV to. After unlocking it, I quickly got in the back seat. Thankfully, the tint was dark. Once he got in with me, he lifted his hips and pulled his pants to his knees and lifted his top. "Come hop on this dick, baby."

I hiked my dress up and at that moment I was glad that it was loose-fitting at the bottom. Quickly straddling him, I slid my thong to the side and slid down his dick to properly thank him for surprising me today. "Ooooh yes, daddy. Take me there."

He gripped my ass while I quickly bounced on his dick. Not wanting to get caught, I just wanted to put us out of our misery. He groaned as he bit his bottom lip, then closed his eyes for a moment. "Fuck, baby. Take me there, too. I feel them legs trembling. Let that shit go."

"Oh... Haji... shit!"

I released and he did at the same time. Once the tremors passed, I leaned my forehead against his. "You so fucking nasty."

"Umm, yo' ass didn't object. I'm gon' tell yo' mama and papa just how much of a freak their daughter is."

I laughed as I practically fell over on the seat next to him. "Damn, girl. Look at all this cream you got on daddy dick. I'm gon' be feeling all moist the rest of the night."

"Just go to the bathroom and clean up, silly. You're the one that pulled me out here. I can't help it that your dick is so good to me that I cum whenever he's inside of me."

That shut his ass up. He smirked, then kissed my lips. "You damn right."

Once we were presentable, he helped me out as Daraja stood at the back door. I could feel my face heating up as we approached her. "Y'all some nasty muthafuckas. Everybody was looking for your asses."

Haji laughed and I did, too, because I'd never heard her use the word y'all. "Shut up and move," I said as I walked past her, pulling Haji with me.

We'd worked up an appetite and I planned to tear some goat up.

As WE SAT out by the pool with my parents and Daraja, we talked about what's been going on with them since I'd been gone, i.e. all the shit they weren't telling me on the phone. We didn't have much time to really talk yesterday. Last night when we left the venue, after bringing my people home, Haji sped all the way to the hotel. He blew my damn back out. Like, literally... my back was killing me this morning. I went downstairs and had a massage. His ass was a whole savage last night. After my massage, we went got my folks and had breakfast in our suite. Once I showed them the pictures of our ceremony in Texas and we'd talked about how we met, we came out to the pool.

Knowing that my mother's health was declining so quickly, I knew I needed to talk to them about moving. I didn't know if they'd made a decision yet or not, but they surely needed to make one soon. "So, Papa, have y'all decided what you were going to do? Are y'all staying here or moving to Texas?"

"I thought we still had time to decide. We're still weighing the pros and cons. That's an extremely long flight. We'd have to purchase new clothes once we got there because we won't be able to take everything."

I rolled my eyes slightly. They were so stuck on being in Lagos. I mean... I got it. They'd lived here all their lives... over fifty years. But why couldn't they see how great the benefits were if they moved in with us? Exhaling loudly, I said, "Okay. We leave in five days. I hope we know by then."

"Papa, please quit playing with her ass. Girl, we're coming! I can't wait!"

My eyebrows lifted and I couldn't believe my ears. I hopped out of my seat and asked, "Really?"

"Yeah, Chi Chi, we're coming."

I hugged my daddy tightly, then my mama. "I'm so excited! I'm about to get in the pool. You coming, Haji?"

He licked his lips as I took off my wrap and said, "Uh-huh."

Just as he stood, his family walked outside. They were staying in the same hotel as us. Ms. Afiong sat next to my mama. They'd gotten acquainted before the wedding yesterday. When I saw Kevin, I kind of shied away from him. I didn't know how genuine he was. After everyone greeted us, he was the last to approach us. "Hey, you two."

"Hi," I responded.

Haji shook his hand as he turned his attention back to me. "I owe you an apology. That wasn't my place. I was being judgmental, jealous, and just evil. I apologize."

He extended his hand to me and I shook it with a slight smile as Haji wrapped his arm around me, resting his hand on my hip. "I accept your apology. Thank you for offering it."

He nodded, then walked away to go sit with the rest of the family. Daraja was already in the water and Taj and Imani had joined her. "Baby, did he say why he's been so mean to you?"

"Yeah. Jealousy and he's not my biological brother. Which, I really need to talk to my mama about. Yesterday was the wedding so I didn't want to bring it up. But I'll talk to her later today before dinner."

"Damn. So, he got preferential treatment because he was adopted?"

"Pretty much."

I shook my head slowly. While there was probably more to the story, that must have been the gist of it. I couldn't understand how they could treat their own flesh and blood like shit. But I suppose that wasn't my business. As we stepped down into the pool, Haji lifted me in his arms. "You know that Nigeria sun hit different. We gon' be black as hell by the time we get out of this water."

I laughed so hard, I almost got choked. "You'll still be my pretty black doll, though."

"That I know, baby. We'll lighten back up eventually," I said, then chuckled. "Thank you for being so wonderful."

"As your husband, I'm supposed to be. You want a drink?"

"It's only eleven. What kind of drink?"

"Looks like frozen drinks."

"I'll pass."

Wiggling out of his arms, I went to his back and wrapped my legs around him, gently kissing his back. "Chinara, I was holding you like I was for a reason. I will give it to you in a pool full of people. I know you don't want that."

"Try me."

He whipped his head around so fast, I couldn't help but die laughing. "Girl, don't play. People gon' think a snake done got in the water."

I laughed more as he flicked droplets of water from his fingers in my face. "I'm gonna go talk to my sister for a moment."

"A'ight, baby. I'm gonna go play with Imani and Fayola so I can keep my mind off what I wanna do to you."

I rolled my eyes playfully. "Nasty."

He laughed as I waded to my sister. I couldn't stop the smile that was on my face. I hadn't been this happy in a long time. Going to

America was bittersweet. While I knew I was going to make life better for my family, I still had to leave them behind. So, actually, I was wrong. This level of happiness was something I'd never felt. My jaw muscles were going to be sore before the day was over. When I got to her, she smiled brightly. She was leaning against the wall of the pool, sipping on a frozen beverage. "I didn't think you'd be able to separate from Haji's fine ass long enough to come talk to me."

"Oh, hush. I'm so excited y'all are coming," I said as I hugged her tightly.

"You! I'm beyond excited. It's been hard trying to take care of Mama. She's so hardheaded."

I frowned. "What do you mean?"

"Well... it's not her being hardheaded, it's more of we can't afford the healthy foods that she's supposed to eat. Because the air is out at home, none of us want to even think of turning on the stove or oven. When you sent the money, I begged her to let me buy her some salads, chicken breast and things like that. She refused because she didn't want to spend so much money on food. Maybe now with us being with you, she can relax. I feel like her diabetes and neuropathy have gotten worse because of stress. She's retaining fluid and has high blood pressure, too."

I rested against the side of the pool beside Daraja. "I'm sorry you've had the bulk of the responsibility taking care of Mama. You deserve this time to figure out what you wanna do for you. What do you wanna do? Do you have a boyfriend here that you're leaving behind?"

"I want to be a nurse. I feel like I'm on the path to that now, helping Mama with her medicine and practically diagnosing her issues before we even get to the doctor. I'm scared to go to school, though. I know that I will, but I have anxiety about it because I've been out of school for seven years. I hope it doesn't take me long to get back in the swing of things. And no, I don't have a boyfriend. Just somebody I kick it with to get orgasms that aren't self-motivated."

I smiled slightly. Draping my arm over her shoulder, I said, "I hate that you were alone in caring for them. I plan to make every minute worth it. You will do well in school as long as you are focused, dedicated, and disciplined. You're definitely smart." I kissed her cheek, then continued, "At least you aren't leaving love behind."

"Taking care of Mama is already worth every minute. She's my mother. But I look forward to following my dreams in America with my big sister." She took a sip of her drink, then said, "I know Haji has some fine-ass friends, right?"

I chuckled and said, "Jarius is his best friend. He was in one of the wedding pictures. He took most of the pictures for us. He's also Haji's barber."

"You'll have to show me his picture again."

"Right now, you just focus on getting in school. Have you applied for your Visa yet?"

"Yeah, for all of us."

"Good."

Haji brought me a frozen drink anyway and immediately noticed the expression on my face. "It's virgin. I'll get you drunk later once everyone retires for the night."

I smirked at him, then said, "Thank you, baby." Taking a sip, I looked back at him and mumbled, "Nasty ass."

Looking at my little sister, I smiled and clinked my glass against hers. "To new beginnings."

 aji

"BECAUSE HE WAS ADOPTED, he got a pass? I'm still confused as to why y'all never told me. What was the point in keeping it from me if Kevin already knew?"

"It was just easier not telling you. We didn't want to have to answer all the questions that you weren't mature enough to handle. I'm sorry, Haji. Kevin was spoiled and I know it was because I felt sorry for him. His mother left him on our doorstep overnight. We didn't find him there until morning. Anything could have happened to him. Finding a dead baby on our doorstep would have killed me. He wasn't a newborn, but still. He was barely ten months old. Any wild animal could have gotten ahold of him."

"But I don't think y'all realized how that affected me, especially Dad. While I was strong-minded and strong-willed, I still needed those pats on the back, those congratulatory moments, saying job well-done, son. It was like nothing I accomplished was good enough.

That hurt. But it also made me not just turn my back on y'all, it made me turn my back on my heritage, my country. While I have no problem telling anyone where I'm from, I tried extra hard to fit in when I got to college. I submerged myself in the culture... especially the southern culture of the country."

I ran my hand down my face as I took a deep breath. She was looking at me like she didn't really understand and that only irritated me. My mother was a smart woman. That was her way of avoiding the conversation. She knew I would get irritated with trying to *make* her understand and just say forget it. That wasn't gonna happen today. I understood why Kevin was coddled and spoiled more, but why did that mean they had to treat me like I didn't belong? "What did what Kevin endured as a baby have to do with me?"

She lowered her head and I knew that meant she was trying to get her thoughts together. My mother was rarely one to fidget. I'd only witnessed her doing that a couple of times my entire life. It was like nothing made her nervous. When she lifted her head, she said, "We overcompensated. We saw the error of our ways with Kevin. Not that I don't love him or that I think less of him, but I knew that he would be attached to me for probably his entire life. I... *we* wanted more for you... better for you. When we learned that you were a rebel, we chose to use reverse psychology on you to get you to do exactly what we wanted you to do."

Well, ain't that some shit. My eyebrows lifted slightly as she continued. "The more we were against you doing something, the more you wanted to do it. We were both all for you going to school in America. While we expected you to come back, we weren't upset that you stayed. You have a good life there and we always wanted what was best for you, Haji. While our parenting style with Kevin made him weak, we wanted you to be strong. We were extremely proud of you and your dad bragged on you to all his colleagues. But we couldn't seem to find a happy medium with the both of you, like we seemed to have with Umaru."

I didn't know what to think. What if the absence of their love would have broken me halfway across the world? What if I would have gotten involved in bullshit that I had no business in? Instead, I did my best to prove that I was worthy, and I still didn't get their love. While Mama was way more affectionate and attentive than Dad, I craved more. "I don't know if I understand that logic or if I even care to understand it. Dad is dead and I'm successful. So, I guess it worked."

"We didn't want you to look at Kevin any differently, but it only seemed to make y'all hate each other. Kevin thought we were gonna forget about him because of you and you felt like we didn't care about you because of how we treated Kevin. We made a difference and didn't see it until it was too late. I'm so sorry."

I nodded and as I stood to leave her hotel room, she asked, "Can I ask you a question?"

Turning back to her, I said, "Yes, ma'am."

"Did you marry Chinara because of the stipulation your dad put on your inheritance?"

Taking a deep breath, I sat next to her, opting to tell her the truth. "I *asked* her to marry me because of that. I was interested in getting to know her before Dad died. What I didn't expect was to fall in love with her so quickly. By the time we got married, I was all in. As crazy as it sounds, I love her more than I've ever loved anybody. So, because my intentions were skewed when I asked her to marry me the first time, I asked her again out of love. I wanted her to experience every-thing a bride is supposed to feel on her wedding day. She means that much to me and I know I mean a lot to her as well."

My mama pulled me in her arms and hugged me tightly. She said repeatedly how proud of me she was and how much she loved me. Feeling her tears against my cheek caused me to pull away from her to peer into her eyes. Gently wiping her cheek, I asked, "Why are you crying?"

"Because we could have really damaged you. While we felt like we knew your personality, we could have broken you. I'm not sure why your dad stipulated that in his will for you, but we will find out soon."

"Six months."

"No. When we get back to the States. I'm going back with you and Chinara. Your dad has a safe deposit box in Houston. That's where your inheritance is. I never expected you to find someone to marry. But it all turned out for the best. You found an irreplaceable love."

I frowned slightly. "So, you could have given me my inheritance without me getting married?"

"No. But I don't have to make you wait six months."

She smiled at me and I smiled back at her. That was a weight lifted off my shoulders. While I wanted to help Chinara's family, I knew that things would eventually get tough if I was spending more than what I had coming in. While I knew her dad would be searching for a job when they got to Texas, that wasn't guaranteed. I nodded and said, "Well, come on, let's go join everyone else for dinner. Thank you, Ma."

"You don't have to thank me, son. I should be thanking you for not writing us off completely. I love you."

"I love you, too. I hate that Dad isn't here to tell me those things himself. What did the autopsy report say anyway?"

"He had an abdominal aneurysm. There would have been nothing they could have done to stop him from bleeding out. Before the aneurysm could fully manifest itself, he had a massive heart attack as well. Turns out, he had health issues that he kept hidden from us all. So, be sure to stay in shape and get checkups, Haji."

"Yes, ma'am."

It felt like the relationship between my mother and me was repaired, but I still couldn't help but wish that I would have had the same opportunity with my dad. He was so damn stubborn.

Like me.

MY NERVES WERE on ten as we traveled to Houston to see exactly what my dad had in store for me within this safety deposit box. After our wedding ceremony in Beaumont, my mama had gotten the key from the attorney. She said she could see how much I loved Chinara even then. Our second wedding ceremony in Nigeria was so lovely, it damn near moved me to tears. Chinara's dress was stunning and she was so beautiful, she really looked like a porcelain doll. The kind you stood up on a shelf and refused to touch. But she got touched in every way imaginable that day. Even after that ceremony, we'd managed to sneak away to a private restroom and get a quickie.

I couldn't get enough of her and she couldn't get enough of me. At every turn, we were making nasty comments to one another, telling the other of all the sexy shit we were gonna do to each other when we got the chance. She was my lil freak and if my mama wasn't with us, I'd stop this car right now and give it to her. She was seated in the backseat and had let my mama take the front. I didn't agree with that, but she insisted and now I knew why. She kept sliding her nails down my neck and doing nasty shit with her tongue in my rearview mirror, teasing the fuck out of me.

We'd gotten back home two days ago and we took yesterday to recuperate from the flight. Her mama was wiped out. My mama kind of helped Chinara and Daraja take care of her. She seemed a whole lot better when we left to come to Houston today. Chinara found her some doctors to see and she had appointments all next week. They also had embassy interviews yesterday. Usually, people waited until they received their visa to come to the country, but we needed to move her mother as soon as possible.

Once we got to Bank of America, my nerves had started to kick in. I couldn't stop wondering about what I would find. I knew there were money and jewels and possibly the keys to the house he spoke of in his will, but I was hoping there were no surprises. When we walked in, we had to be seated to wait for a representative to open the vault for us. Just more time for my nerves to be on edge. Chinara grabbed my hand and asked softly in my ear, "Do I need to take you to the restroom?"

I smirked at her, then leaned in close to her ear and gently grabbed her lobe with my teeth. "I'm always down for that shit. You know that."

"Ms. A... bim... bola?"

"Yes."

The rep smiled, then said, "Please follow me."

The three of us stood and followed her behind the caged door to the safety deposit box. Dad had a pretty big box compared to the sizes we passed when we first entered the vault. As the woman began pulling it out, she said, "Oh. It's heavy. Can you help me?"

I nodded, then helped her pull the box out and sit it on the table. "Thank you. One of you let me know when you're done?"

"Yes, ma'am, we will," my mama responded.

The lady left out, locking us inside so no one else could come in while we were back there. My mama inserted the key in the box, her hand steady as hell. When she turned it, the top sprang open like it was a lot of shit in there. Glancing back up at her, she smiled at me and said, "Go ahead, Haji."

With a trembling hand, I flipped the lid up and my lips parted slightly. I could see cash, but I went straight to the envelope on top. When I grabbed it, I noticed there was another envelope beneath it. Quickly opening it, there was a letter. I had been hoping there would be some explanation as to why he did the things he did and hopefully, this letter would explain it all. There were two slips of paper. When I opened the first one, in his handwriting it read, *I love you more than life, son.*

Swallowing the lump in my throat, a couple of tears dropped in the process. I didn't realize just how much it would mean to me to have heard him say that. If only a letter had me like this, then I could imagine the effect it would have had on me had he said it while he was living. Chinara gently wiped my cheek as I smiled tightly at her.

Setting it to the side, I unfolded the next piece of paper. It was a much longer letter.

HAJI,

Let me start by saying you are my pride and joy. Although I didn't show it to you, everyone I dealt with in all of Salone knew just how much you meant to me. I would have moved heaven and earth for you. I was extremely hard on you and I apologize. My intent was to make sure you would be strong enough to face the challenges you would face in the world. I knew you were destined for great things and I wanted you to be able to handle it mentally. I rejoiced for every graduation and every milestone you surpassed. I hate that I didn't show you how proud I was. I hope you can forgive me.

SETTING the letter down for a moment, I allowed the tears to continue falling. This was the validation I needed from him. To know that he was so proud of me was healing to my wounded soul. After wiping my face, I continued reading.

ALONG WITH THE money and jewels you see in the box, I left my business to you and your brothers. You have the option to sell your portion because you are so far away. I also know that you wanted no parts of the mines. To make sure they don't try to cheat you, the business is worth 3.3 billion dollars.

Now, you're probably wondering why I placed a stipulation on your inheritance. Just because you were in another country, didn't mean that I didn't have people checking in on you. But I'm sure you already know that from the letter the lawyer gave you. The reckless way you were sleeping around with so many women, I knew it was because you were searching for something that I didn't give you. My *stipulation was to hopefully help you find the one. The woman that would move your soul.*

There was a clause in the will that if you hadn't found your ONE within a year that you would be granted your inheritance. I never wanted to keep what was yours from you. Besides that aspect of life, you presented yourself as a responsible adult. I suppose you were somewhat responsible in that area as well, since you didn't have children all over the place.

Enjoy your money and wealth, son. For the trouble, I left you an extra million. Don't tell your brothers. I feel like my legacy will live on through you, but don't make the same mistakes I made with your children. Be firm but show them love, too. I love you so much and again, I'm sorry for making you feel unworthy.

Your proud father,
Ense Abimbola

P.S.- THE KEYS and address to your estate are in the bag with the jewels.

WHEN I FINISHED READING, I had to sit for a moment with my thoughts. It was a lot to digest. To be able to accept his love after he was no longer here was difficult. I didn't want to have to finally grieve his absence, but I succumbed. The emotions I should have felt when he died all bombarded me at once and I found myself crying audibly for the first time as an adult. Chinara rushed over to me and hugged me tightly as my mama smiled. I believed she knew everything that letter said, but she would never admit that to me.

After pulling myself together, I went back to the box. When I opened the other envelope, there were eight cashier's checks, each two hundred fifty thousand dollars. Most banks only insured accounts up to that amount, so I understood why he split the money that way. There was also twenty thousand in cash and a black velvet bag that contained diamonds and nuggets of gold. The keys to my new house was in there as well, just as he stated. I was so overwhelmed, I just stood there for a moment. Chinara walked over to me and asked, "You okay, baby?"

"Yeah. Let's put this in your purse and get out of here."

As my mama approached, I pulled her in my arms and hugged her tightly. Feeling the tremble, I knew she was somewhat sensitive right now. This was the man she'd loved for over forty years. "Thank you for bringing me here. It gave me closure and a new respect for my father. It also help me release forgiveness for him. I love you."

"Love you more, baby."

Once we got everything in Chinara's purse, we went to the car and headed for the residence. It took us about twenty minutes to get there, but when we did, all of us were stunned. I parked in front of the gate, then stared at the paper to make sure I'd put the address in correctly. It was huge. After putting the code in for the gate to open, we drove up the cobblestone road to the front door. We were all silent as we sat there, frozen in place from shock.

When I finally gathered the gall, I stepped out of the car. Chinara did as well, then walked around and handed me the keys. Looking down at the paper with the address on it, I realized it was folded. After opening it, I saw the home's description: *8 bd / 12 ba / 26,401 sqft / 2.5 acres*

What was I gonna do with this much house? Walking to the door, I unlocked it and retrieved the security code from the paper as well. Once the security system was disarmed, we walked through the fully furnished house in wonder. Three families could live here and not notice one another. As Mama detoured taking her own tour, I brought Chinara into the nearest bedroom. Pushing her against the wall, I quickly pulled her pants down, then freed my dick. I could no longer contain my emotions and I knew the best way to free them would be in her gushy-ass pussy. "Haji..." she whispered. "What are you doing?"

"Quit tripping. You know you want this shit as badly as I do.

Seeing all this shit I just inherited, I need to get some of this energy off me."

Picking her up, I slid her down my pole, then collided into the wall. Hopefully, she was okay afterwards. During the moment, nothing seemed to hurt her. I couldn't help but be rough, though. My adrenaline was pumping through me like a basketball player on a fast-break. "Oh, fuck!" I yelled. "I'm glad this pussy mine."

"Haji... yes. Rewrite your name on it and through it, daddy."

As I gripped her ass, I slammed her on all my inches repeatedly as she screamed my name. Her juices had leaked down my balls to my thighs and I didn't plan to stop until that shit had rolled down to my ankles. Her pussy was sweetly serenading me with its sloshing noises and it only made me get nastier with her. As I held her ass in my hands, literally and figuratively, I slid a finger in her wet asshole. Stroking it as I stroked her pussy proved to be something she liked because her screams were no longer contained.

I'd learned that a time or two before now. She was recklessly yelling obscenities like we were the only ones in the house. But I didn't give a fuck. All I cared about was pleasing her... killing that pussy... taking her soul to commune with mine. "Ahh fuck! Chinara, you so fucking wet. I can't wait to do all kinds of nasty shit to you in this house."

"Yes, daddy. Take your... pussy. Do with it... as you please."

"Uh-huh. What about this ass, though? Can I do with it as I please, too?"

"Yes, baby. Just... not... noooowww!" she screamed as she came.

Feeling her juices really coat my dick was enough to drive me insane. It was like I was a wild animal that she gave a raw piece of meat to. My teeth sank into her shoulder as I lifted my arms, causing her knees to reach her shoulders as well. Watching my dick going in and out of her, dripping her juices to the floor, gave me chills. Knowing that she was willing to explore sexually with me, was another high she'd placed me on, and I couldn't wait to experience new heights with her.

When my body began trembling, I knew this nut was gonna be earth-shattering. "Oh fuck, baby! Ahhh!" I growled as my shit shot off, causing my knees to buckle.

Stroking through my release made that shit last longer and I wasn't mad about it. As I caught my breath, I allowed her legs to slide from my arms. We were both drained but still craving one another. My dick still had a lil aggression in him, and I knew her pussy could use another round. Surprisingly, we'd gone three days without sex. "I know I put a baby in you that time."

"You put a baby in me already, Haji."

I frowned as I stared at her, as I continued to try to catch my breath. "What?"

"I'm pregnant. I took a test when we got back from Lagos. My period was a few days late and it's always on time."

"I'm gonna be a daddy?"

She smiled at me, excitement in her eyes, as she nodded, then lowered her head. Quickly grabbing her face, I kissed her lips, then rested my forehead against hers. "Pretty Black Doll, you've made me the happiest man alive. Thank you for being my queen."

After kissing her again, we got our pants on, then she headed in the direction my mama was yelling. Standing in the room, admiring the detail of the ceilings, I stared a little longer. Realizing that everything happened for a reason, I came to the conclusion, that had it not been for my dad, I wouldn't be living here with my forever... my pretty black doll. "Thank you, Dad and I love you, too."

EPILOGUE

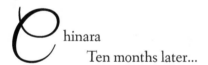hinara
            Ten months later...

"YOUR PRINCESS IS SO BEAUTIFUL," Daraja said.

"Princess is right. I feel like I'm in a damn castle when I come here. Who needs this much house for five people... well, six now?" Jarius asked sarcastically.

Daraja rolled her eyes as she continued to rock our two-month-old baby girl named Jendayi. Her name meant grateful and thankful. We were definitely that when she graced this world with her presence. Being almost nine pounds when I delivered her, I thought I was dying. But somehow, I managed after only six hours of labor. The nurse said I'd labored some at home without knowing it. I'd dilated five centimeters before I got there, but I hadn't lost my mucus plug and my water was still intact. However, the minute they broke it, all hell broke loose only for heaven to emerge from it.

Haji was beyond smitten with his princess. So much so, until he didn't start fiending for sex until Jendayi was five weeks old. He was waking up more than I was to feed her milk I'd pumped, although he was still working. He'd gotten a job at a chemical plant here in Houston after we'd been here a couple of months. Our lives were busy. He didn't sell his portion of his father's business. Instead, he handled the business side of it with buyers from the U.S. His brothers handled the other countries. The companies here in the U.S. were their biggest partners. His brothers knew he would do a better job at managing that. Frankly, I didn't know where he found the time.

My parents were living with us and they'd been granted citizenship, along with Daraja. She was going to University of Houston to become a nurse, just as she'd planned. She finished her first semester with a 4.0 GPA. I knew she would do well. She still didn't have a boyfriend, though, and wasn't the least bit concerned about getting one. Jarius was interested in her, but she wasn't feeling him like that. At least that was what she said. I'd seen her face redden slightly on more than one occasion when he was here. Being that she was lighter complexioned than me, it was easier to see her blush.

Mama's health was so much better now that we'd gotten her hooked up with a group of doctors at Methodist Hospital. We'd had to take her to ER a couple of weeks after we'd gotten here to find out her blood pressure was extremely high. Thankfully, we'd gotten her there before anything major happened. We'd gotten her in a water aerobics class, and she was moving around a lot better. She rarely had to use a cane. Her sugars were controlled, and her nerve damage hadn't gotten any worse.

Since Haji had so much money now, he told my dad not to worry about finding a job, just to enjoy time with my mama. And that was what he did... after much objection, though. He'd put in a few applications for janitors and security guards, but no one called him. Haji told him that was because he needed to quit being stubborn and just enjoy life. After a couple of months had passed without a call back, he finally gave in to Haji's suggestion and began water aerobics with Mama.

I'd found my niche in communications by modeling for a couple of ads for a local boutique, then for the store Motherhood while I was pregnant. So, my face was on TV, just as I'd hoped. Haji was extremely protective after that, thinking I was a star. I couldn't help but laugh at him. Our marriage was going well, and our first anniversary was this coming weekend. Haji had promised that we would do something special to celebrate. The past two months had been totally about Jendayi.

After Jarius left me and Daraja alone, I said, "You know you want that man. I don't know why you just don't give in. He's in Houston almost every Sunday and Monday. I know he don't miss Haji that damn much."

"I ain't got time for Jarius right now."

"Oh, right now? So that means maybe in the near future?"

She side-eyed me and continued to slowly rock Jendayi. She'd begun to whine a bit, so I knew it was time to feed her. Since I was breastfeeding, she handed her over to me. There was no shame in my game, either. No matter who was around, I would pop my breast out and feed my baby. Haji almost had a heart attack when him and Jarius walked in the house with me in the kitchen pulling my boob out. He'd said Jarius had no business seeing his pleasure bags. I laughed so damn loud, I scared the baby. She wouldn't nurse for a whole thirty minutes after that.

"I had sex with him, Chinara."

"What!" I yelled, feeling Jendayi flinch in my arms.

She took a deep breath and said, "We fucked, and it was so damn good. I have shit to accomplish, though. If I keep messing around with his ass, I'm gon' get caught up for sure. And he's so damn fine."

"Well, don't be too hard on yourself to where it causes you to miss out on something special. I almost missed out on one of the best things to ever happen to me. It's possible to be in love and finish school."

"I know, I know. I'm trying to make sure this is something I want. I don't want to date him if it's just lust. We can just continue fucking if that's the case. Most of the shit he says gets on my nerves. He probably does that shit on purpose just to make up with me."

"How many times have y'all slept together?"

"A few times. But change the subject. I'll think about it."

I rolled my eyes and continued nursing my baby, enjoying my role in this family. Verizon finally called me not long after we'd gotten back from Nigeria. I had to tell them I was no longer available. I'd accepted a position that their pay and benefits couldn't touch. Being Haji's wife, concubine, baby mama, private dancer, and sometimes his escort when we were role-playing, had surpassed even my own dreams of what having a husband would be like. And now that we'd started a family, there was nothing else that could top that.

While burping Jendayi, Haji walked into the room. Before he could get to us, she let out a huge burp, causing me and Daraja to giggle. Haji chuckled, then grabbed his princess from me and said, "Me and my chocolate princess about to go swimming. Y'all coming?"

"You have her swimsuit?"

"Yep. It's on the patio. Now that she's had her immunizations, baby girl finna be exposed to a world she's never known."

"Just like her mama. I love you, Haji Okiro Abimbola, with my heart and soul."

"I love you, too, Pretty Black Doll. So much so, I had to marry you twice."

THE END

AFTERWORD

From the Author

So... this story was different... as in the proposal of marriage part of it for me. However, the hot scenes were there, and I was beyond excited whenever these two would come together. That first scene of them masturbating in separate rooms... OMG! Haji was definitely book bae material and I loved him! I hope you enjoyed the story as much as I enjoyed writing it.

There's also an amazing playlist on Apple Music and Spotify for this book under the same title that includes some great R&B and rap tracks to tickle your fancy. Please keep up with me on Facebook (@authormonicawalters), Instagram (@authormonicawalters) and Twitter (@monlwalters). You can also visit my Amazon author page at www.amazon.com/author/monica.walters to view my releases. Please subscribe to my webpage for updates! https://authormonicawalters.com.

For live discussions, giveaways, and inside information on upcoming releases, join my Facebook group, Monica's Romantic Sweet Spot at https://bit.ly/2P2lo6X.

You Belong to Me

The Shorts: A BLP Anthology with the Authors of BLP

All I Need is You (A crossover novel with Divine Love by T. Key)

Until I Met You

Behind Closed Doors Series

Be Careful What You Wish For

You Just Might Get It

Show Me You Still Want It

Sweet Series

Bitter Sweet

Sweet and Sour

Sweeter Than Before

Sweet Revenge

Sweet Surrender

Sweet Temptation

Sweet Misery

Sweet Exhale

Motives and Betrayal Series

Ulterior Motives

Ultimate Betrayal

Ultimatum: #lovemeorleaveme, Part 1

Ultimatum: #lovemeorleaveme, Part 2

Written Between the Pages Series

The Devil Goes to Church Too

The Book of Noah (A Crossover Novel with The Flow of Jah's Heart by

T. Key)

The Revelations of Ryan, Jr. (A Crossover Novel with All That Jazz by T. Key)

Coming Soon:

Nobody Else Gon' Get My Love (A Crossover Novel with Better Than Before by T. Key)